Sea Glass and Salt Air

By Micaela Nicolini

You deserve all the good things! ♥

♥ Micaela Nicolini

ISBN:

To all the loves that have held my heart
You shaped me, and shaped this book

Table of Contents

CHAPTER ONE

The Quiet Things That No One Ever Knows -- Brand New

Rosario considered herself to be many things--awkward, kind, genuine--but she never thought of herself as shallow. Honestly, she really believed that. But...before her stood the very definition of her perfect guy. He was tall—over six feet—with dark black hair that swept down in front of his bright blue eyes. His long fingers splayed across his broad chest as he threw back his head and laughed. A semi-circle of enraptured faces were arranged around him in a post-Church service crowd. Rosario felt as captivated as they looked.

"Rosie?" A hand flew in front of her face, back and forth, before she blinked away her stupor.

"Yeah, sorry..." She smiled sheepishly.

The girl in front of her—Taylor, maybe?—had volunteered to show her around the church after service and get her acquainted with everything. Rosario was new to the town. Her whole family had moved right at the tail end of summer, uprooting her from all her familiar haunts. She had resigned herself to leave as soon as she received her college acceptance letter from Mt. Saint Mary's in the spring, but Rosario hadn't anticipated her whole family following her. Her mom called it a blessing that her new job brought her to the town where Rosario would be going to school, but Rosario couldn't quite bring herself to agree.

The new move brought her to a brand new church. Back in Mooreland, her hometown, Rosario went to a contemporary church full of low lighting, guitar-riff laden worship and no dress code. Her old church was full to bursting. Their Sunday services took place in a converted warehouse, each aisle created out of rows and rows of collapsible seating.

This new church was a legitimate church building with courtyards and kids classrooms and an honest to God steeple. The congregation in its entirety had to amount to less than a few hundred, but they milled about in tight-knit groups that spoke to having a kind of community Rosario had never come across before. This church had a much more... classic feel. An anxious sweat prickled the back of her neck as she shifted from foot to foot.

Rosario knew that tuning out a would-be friend in favor of ogling some guy - in a church no less - was a pretty crappy way of starting things, but she hoped the girl who was probably named Taylor would accept any weirdness as a byproduct of her newness, and not as a visceral reaction to laying eyes on a tall lanky blue eyed boy who so instantly zinged through her being.

"Oh! Let me introduce you!" The girl who might not be Taylor obviously picked up on her stare and led Rosario toward the group of people clustered around the tall guy Rosario needed to stop checking out. Hopefully, maybe Taylor didn't pick up on her blush.

"Guys." Taylor pulled Rosario by the hand to the middle of the cluster of people. "This is Rosario, she's new to the church."

"You can call me Ro if you want." She gave the group her most winning smile.

"I thought I heard your mom call you Rosie?" Taylor asked, her head cocked to the side. The blush that had finally calmed down after ogling the hot guy flared up again. Rosie had once been a familial nickname, but others in her life had taken to calling her by it and eventually it just served to make her feel small and childish. *Not a great way to start out here at Northwest church.*

"Wow Tay, way to call her out!" said the boy to Rosario's left. He was tall, though not as tall as the guy that originally caught her eye, with sandy blonde hair and wire-rimmed glasses. "I'm Scott, it's nice to meet you, Ro."

"Nice to meet you too." Rosario shuffled her feet nervously.

Taylor (her name was definitely Taylor) went on to introduce the rest of the group. There was Nancy, a tall, slender preschool teacher's aide. Paul, a Korean student with a giant smile. Kathryn, the worship team lead singer. Ro immediately noticed they were practically a study in opposites. Where Kathryn was thin and athletic Rosario was soft and curvy. Kathryn had a full face of pristine make-up and bright open eyes where Rosario had a naked face boxed in by thick black framed glasses. Kathryn was average height with a long, elegant neck that was accentuated by her angular bob. Ro had a round face settled closer to her chest encompassed in a thick, wavy mess of jet black hair. But the most striking thing about Kathryn was the way she held herself—as if she knew her features caused you to look twice and she was comfortable with the weight of those extra glances. Meanwhile Rosario shied away from any notice at all.

"And this is Michael." Taylor smiled up at the guy that originally drew Rosario's eye.

For the first time, Rosario met his gaze and instantly the shocking blue of his eyes swallowed her up. Their eyes held one another for a few beats before Rosario had to look away, overcome by the instinctive tug of attraction it pulled from her mind. As she pulled her gaze away, she gave him a hopefully covert once over. He was devastatingly handsome in faded skinny jeans, chucks, and a band t-shirt.

"Oh, Motion City Soundtrack! That's my all-time favorite band!" A grin lit up Rosario's face, her previous embarrassment forgotten.

"Whoa, really?" Michael fixed her with a strange look.

"Yeah, for sure. I got to see them in concert once. It was a great show." Rosario couldn't help the excitement that crept into her voice. The smile that lit up her face was no longer shy, just genuinely bursting forth with enthusiasm.

The confusion in Michael's face took on a softness as he smiled down at her.

"That's awesome. I really like them too." His tone was fond and warm.

Rosario felt herself shying away from his searching gaze.

"I don't know about you guys, but I'm starving." Scott clapped a hand to his stomach to emphasize his point. "Why don't we all meet up at the Mesa and grab something to eat?"

"The Mesa?" Rosario asked.

"Yeah, it's this shopping mall. It's a few blocks down from the beach, but you've got to walk all the way down this hill to really get to the water," Taylor explained. "I can drive you over there if you want."

"Yeah, please. That'd be great." Rosario jumped on the chance to hitch a ride with someone else. She'd carpooled with her family to the service and the thought of them dropping her off made her feel uncomfortably childish. She was weeks away from turning eighteen, right in that limbo between teen and adult, and getting babied in front of these people would make her die a little on the inside. She couldn't be sure, but by looks alone she figured she was the youngest one of the bunch.

"Cool, let's head out then," Scott said. The group dispersed with a few hollered goodbyes as they walked to their separate rides. Taylor whipped out her car keys and stopped beside a truly adorable silver VW bug. Rosario smiled, knowing from the short time she'd met Taylor that this car was perfectly fitting for its owner. She unlocked the car and slid behind the driver's seat.

At the turn of the key Ke$ha came blasting out of the speakers at an eardrum rattling volume. Rosario winced, barely stopping herself from clapping her hands to her ears.

"Sorry," Taylor laughed and turned down the volume to a whisper. "I like to get pumped up in the morning, and right now Ke$ha is what does it for me."

"I can respect that." Rosario nodded and buckled in.

"Really?" Taylor looked relieved. "Everyone else gives me such a hard time for loving Ke$ha, and since you were all into that band Michael likes I was worried you'd tease me too."

"No way," Rosario smiled reassuringly. "I love all kinds of music. In fact, if you were streaming my last playlist it'd be full of K-Pop, which is Korean pop music."

"Really?" Now Taylor seemed to be holding back judgment. "Do you speak Korean?"

"Nah, but that doesn't mean I can't like the music."

Taylor pulled out of the small church parking lot with an ease that spoke of lots of repetition.

"How long have you been going to this church?" Rosario asked.

"Oh man, probably ten years now," Taylor responded.

"Woah, really? That's nuts."

"Yeah, well, considering the fact that I'm twenty-one it sounds a lot more impressive than it is. I started going to this place because Michael invited basically everyone in his fifth grade class to this camping weekend. After that, the church kind of took us all in. The youth program wasn't really a thing at the time, so we made it up as we went along. And now Michael runs the whole show."

"He does?" Rosario asked. She tucked away Taylor's age for future reference and wondered how old that made Michael.

"Yeah, he's the youth pastor. Didn't I tell you that?"

"Uh, maybe?" Rosario had to fight off another blush. It was probably something she mentioned while Rosario had been checking out Michael. Knowing that he was a pastor made her ogling feel extra sinful. "I might have missed a few things."

"Don't worry about it." Taylor glanced away from the road to fix Rosario with a reassuring smile. "I can kind of go overboard sometimes. If it ever gets overwhelming, just let me know and I'll try and rein it in."

"I'll be sure to do that," Rosario responded with a chuckle.

As they crested a hill the ocean came into view, the blue waters melding seamlessly with the sky at the horizon line. She still wasn't used to being so near to the water. Rosario had grown up in Mooreland which was a farming community, surrounded on all sides by fields of onions and citrus trees. The salty ocean breeze was a nice change of pace from the dusty air she was used to.

Taylor pulled into a parking garage and slid into a narrow spot near an escalator. They took that to the surface, sunlight spilling across them as they came up from the underground. She stopped to scan the crowd before Taylor lifted her arm up to wave. Through a small sea of bodies, Rosario spotted Scott at the head of a big, round, metal table covered by a large bright blue umbrella. Rosario reached out to grab Taylor's wrist as they wound through the crowd. Taylor looked back and laughed.

"Nervous about getting lost?"

"Maybe." Rosario laughed.

Scott leaned back in his chair, arms up, hands linked behind his head. "Ladies." He winked at them. "Go find something to eat, Michael is out fetching my food for me while I bravely fight off the hungry crowds."

"You're my hero." Taylor rolled her eyes. "Ro, I can show you a few of the options we've got around here if you want."

"Or you could just go for the best thing around and hit up Blue C."

"What's that?"

"It's this Japanese food place. It's got great sushi and bento boxes that are a pretty good deal."

"Oh man, that sounds awesome." Rosario's mouth began to water. "Where is that?"

"Here, just follow me." Taylor led the way toward a different branching path, past more crowded tables, to a row of shops. Blue C was nestled between a crowded coffee shop and a Pizza Hut. "I'm going to head back toward our table, there's a really great burger place over there. Think you can find your way back?"

"Maybe. You might have to send someone to look for me if I'm gone too long."

With one final goodbye, they split apart and Rosario walked into the packed restaurant. She hung back to peruse the options, her gaze drifting across rows of sushi names and bento combinations. Everything sounded delicious and she couldn't figure out if that told more about her hunger level or the quality of the restaurant.

"You should try the classic bento."

Rosario jolted and turned sharply on her heel, coming face to face with Michael. He stood a scant few inches away from her, a surprised smile spread across his face.

"Woah, sorry, I didn't mean to surprise you," he said.

"You scared me." Rosario prayed her blush wasn't as bright as it felt.

"Didn't mean to," Michael repeated. He took a step back and Rosario swore she could feel the air cool between them. "But really, you should get that bento. It's a great way to get acquainted with the place. It's all the greatest hits."

"Uh, yeah, sure. I think I might do that," Rosario responded. She was suddenly very aware of the fact that this was the first interaction they'd had with just the two of them and she had blown it by being all weird and skittish--she hated that the things in her past had made her this way. Her gaze skipped across the room, looking for a distraction.

"Hey, no pressure. You can't go wrong with the sushi here either."

Rosario's anxiety slipped away at his gentle tone. She never reacted like this to anyone. Rosario reasoned that it was hard to be objective about such a thing, but she was no stranger to relationships and flirting. But for some reason just being around Michael took her off-center, kept her stumbling.

"No, the bento sounds great." Rosario smiled and stepped away from Michael to walk up to the counter. She placed her order and paid, stuffing her change into the tip jar before walking back over to where Michael waited. He was already holding a tray of food but he made no move to leave.

"You don't have to wait for me, you know."

"I know." His smile got a bit wider. "But Scott can wait for a minute."

Rosario got the distinct feeling that Scott got a bit of teasing from the group all around. Then again, maybe they all teased each other like this. Their dynamic was so ingrained that she felt at a loss as to how to continue. A silence stretched between the two of them as Rosario got lost in her own thoughts.

"Where are you?" Michael asked.

"Huh?" Rosario blinked up at him, meeting his bright blue gaze, breathless at the sight.

"Just now, where did you go?" To Rosario his voice sounded soft and fond, but some part of her brain kept reminding her that it was too early to get a read on someone. He probably thought she was just being weird, making fun of her somehow.

"OH, that...ha." She ran her hand through her long, wavy hair in an anxious swipe, tugging at the ends as she spoke. "Nothing, just thinking."

Michael gave her a weighty look and hummed.

"So, Rosario, I need to know--Team Cap or Team Iron Man?"

"Team Cap, definitely," Rosario responded instantly.

Michael's eyes lit up and Rosario preened under his approving gaze.

"Why not Iron Man?"

"Are you kidding? I'm not okay with letting another shady government organization have so much control after what Hydra did."

"Okay but isn't that a little bit alarmist? Can't you trust the government again?" Michael's voice took on a playful lilt.

"Not really, I'd rather put my faith in Steve Roger's tactical mind and good heart."

"That's fair, but—" Before Michael could finish a man popped out from the kitchen, bag in hand.

"Michael, who is your friend?" he asked as he handed the bag off to Rosario.

"This is Ro. She's new in town."

"Ro, it's nice to meet you. I'm Sean; I own the place. Michael here basically keeps me in business." Sean smiled and clapped Michael on the shoulder. "It's nice to see him bringing someone new around the place."

"Everyone else is here too, Sean," Michael said quickly. "It's just that it's so busy outside that they couldn't come in. They're out there saving us a table."

"Yeah, it gets like that at the tail end of the summer around here," Sean let Ro know. "Before you know it it'll be fall and all these tourists will be back at home. Then you'll have the run of the place again." Sean turned his attention to Rosario.

"I'll be seeing you next Sunday, right?" Sean asked with a smile.

"Yeah, definitely." Ro lifted her bag a bit to wave goodbye. She followed Michael back out into the sunny breezeway.

He led her through the throngs of people back to where Sean and the rest of their group were sitting. When they got to the table, Michael pulled out her seat.

Ro froze for a moment, struck suddenly by the thought that the last person to pull out her chair had been her father at one of the father-daughter dances he brought her to as a girl scout.

Michael moved past her and took a seat at the opposite end of the table near Kathryn. The table wasn't big enough to fit them all so Michael had to crowd in close to her and a small part of Ro couldn't help but notice how nice they looked together. They fit. It made something petty in her rise up and take notice.

Rosario shook her head and sat down. She took out the tray of food. Opening it up assaulted her nose with a heavenly smell. Her face must have lit up because from across the table Michael laughed.

"Trust me, it's even better than it looks." Michael nodded before rejoining the group conversation.

Ro took her first bite and let the rhythm of the chatter wash over her. The day was finally catching up with her—all the newness of it made it feel surreal until this grounding moment. This was her new home, these were the new faces she was going to see every week—maybe more.

Suddenly the thought of all she had left behind bloomed up and overshadowed her budding love of this new life. She had been torn away from all of the places that held marks of her growing up—the taqueria down the street where the owner was childhood friends with her mother, the park with the tree she carved her initials into, the locker at her old high school that she'd plastered with stickers. It was all so far away now, not only in distance but in time. And that gap would just keep on growing.

"Ro?" Taylor called, waving a hand in front of her face. "Hey, can you move? I keep hitting Paul with my elbow."

"Yeah, sorry, here, let me—" Ro stood up and pulled her chair down the length of the table with an ear-splitting grind of metal on concrete. The area fell into a momentary silence at the sound, but before Rosario could even bring herself to be embarrassed, new chatter spilled into the silence and filled it back to bursting.

"So Rosario, tell us a little about yourself," Paul called from his side of the table. He'd had excellent timing—Ro had just shoved a rather large piece of sushi into her mouth. She held up a finger and quickly chewed. The group eyed her with clear amusement and Rosario couldn't help but think Paul had timed this on purpose.

"Not much to tell. I'm new here because my mom got a new job, but I would have been here regardless in a few weeks, since I'm starting at Mount St. Mary's this fall."

"Oh really?" Kathryn asked. "That's where Michael went to school."

"Yup. I think you'll really like it there," Michael said, mouth full of food. "It's got this amazing lush campus--greenery everywhere! Man, I still miss it sometimes."

"It's really beautiful up there in the mountains," Nancy added. She'd only said a word here or there, but her face lit up at the mention of the school. "There are some great hiking trails nearby—totally scenic. Michael goes about every week. Hey! We should all go sometime."

"Yeah, maybe." Rosario freaked out internally. She could barely walk up stairs without getting winded. The thought of trudging up a mountain—however beautiful—with these new people outpacing her made her cringe, especially if Michael was apparently a regular at the place.

"Don't worry, the most beautiful hike is pretty easy" Nancy reassured her. "It brings you through the woods to this little waterfall. The water is always freezing though, so I wouldn't suggest jumping in."

"The water is crazy shallow anyway," Michael cut in, mouth now free of food.

"Michael's just saying that because he hates the thought of having all that 'dirty' water anywhere near his body," Scott stage whispered. He was at the other end of the table from Rosario, so everyone heard him.

"Hey, leave him alone," Kathryn glared at Scott. "He doesn't have to like it."

"Anyway! We should all go. And go before all the other students get into town and ruin everything." Taylor aimed a wink at Rosario.

"Okay." Rosario let out a breath, reassured by Taylor's words. "Yeah, let's do it."

CHAPTER TWO

"Broken Heart" -- Motion City Soundtrack

Rosario came home feeling lighter, buoyed up by the happiness from a day full of new friends. Her phone was full of everyone's phone numbers. When Michael had added his number into her contacts her heart had skipped a beat, excited for future conversations they might have. She picked past empty boxes on the way to her room.

The house her family had moved to was *small.*

Back in Mooreland they had lived in a sprawling 3600 square foot home. One side of the house held the rooms for her and her brother Israel, then there was a large kitchen and living area, then an open office and on the second floor her parents had their own closed off suite. But living in Mooreland had been cheap, and the beach side town of Coast Village had a much bigger price tag. So they had moved into an adorable -- but small -- condo. The entryway was shallow, veering sharply in one direction to a converted garage space while the other direction led to steep stairs. Up on the main floor there was a living room, tiny galley kitchen, two bedrooms, and one bathroom.

Since she was moving out soon, Rosario had been relegated to living in the converted garage space. It mostly held a washer and dryer, but they had also managed to fit in a pull out couch that barely cleared the space provided. It was lumpy and it smelled kind of funny, but Rosario was the kind of person that could sleep anywhere. Planes, cars, even in class. It was a blessing, but also a curse, because when she felt tired it was impossible to keep herself awake without the help of caffeine.

Her mother was doing laundry when Rosario walked in and flopped down on the (not pulled out) couch.

"How was lunch?" her mother asked as she moved a load of towels from the washer into the dryer. With the press of a few buttons, the dryer hummed to life, so Rosario raised her voice over the buzz.

"It was great, actually. We had a good time. I've got plans to go hiking with them all later this week."

"Hiking? Really?" Her mother raised an eyebrow at her.

"I know! Me, hiking. But they said the trail was easy. It's up by the school."

"We should really explore up there a bit before school starts. Marlee, you know, Michael's mom? She told me there was a nice breakfast spot in town nearby. We could head out early tomorrow before I have to go to work."

"Ugh, mom, a morning drive?"

"We'll get coffee afterward. I think you can manage to stay awake that long."

"Alright," Rosario smiled into her pillow, secretly pleased that her mother was excited enough about her new school to make time for her before work. As a kid she'd always loved the times her mother would sneak her out of the house early to go have breakfast at Lorraine's, the local mom and pop diner. It became a family haunt, eventually Lorraine herself saved them their same stools at the counter top. But as Rosario got older and her mother got busier their morning trips stopped.

At her old job, mom had worked her way up into management which had slowly taken up more and more of her time. Rosario would always have the memories of her mother picking her up from school and sitting around the dinner table doing homework with her. But, as she got busier, Rosario picked up Israel and helped them with his homework. Though she couldn't be sure, Ro thought that the reason for her mother's new job and their subsequent move was to help her mother change the pace of her life. Now she seemed to get off of work at a time that allowed her to be home with all of them. Sure, their lives were currently filled with unpacking and eating pizza straight from the box, but they were definitely together more often and that made Ro happy to endure it all. But she could do without pizza for a while.

Rosario sat up and leaned over the back of the couch to grab her laptop. She had taken to hiding it around the house ever since she'd caught her little brother balancing it on top of the sink while he was watching some cooking video on YouTube. It would be just her luck to have the laptop she'd spent a year saving for take a bath right before she really needed it.

As her laptop woke up she saw a few notifications trickle in. A few emails caught her eye—she had a few new followers on tumblr, new comments on her Captain America fanfiction, and an email from Mount St. Marys. Something about seeing such an official email with all that other stuff made her laugh, but as she opened up the email her laughter died in her chest. It was an email from the counseling center confirming her appointment for the first week of classes with one of the therapists in the Wellness Center.

"Mom," Rosario tried her best to keep the annoyance out of her voice. "Did you sign me up for counseling?" Her mother stopped shoving a load of dark fabrics into the dryer and turned to look her in the eye. Rosario could see the same look of caution she wore mirrored in her mother's face. Growing up everyone had said Rosario looked more like her father, her mother had light skin and straight jet black hair, but as she grew up she mirrored her mother more and more.

"Yes, Rosie, I did. Now I know what you're going to say—"

"Mom, how did you even do this? You can't just make appointments for me!"

"The website is very intuitive, you just put in your student identification number and—"

"Oh my God, Mom. I can't believe this." Rosario shoved her laptop off her lap and jumped to her feet. "I told you, I don't want to talk to anyone about anything."

"I just thought after the way you left things, you could benefit from venting." Her mother's voice softened, and she grabbed one of Rosario's hands in both of her own. "Honey, when you came home that way looking the way that you did, I was scared out of my mind. I don't know if it's because you didn't have your father around growing up, but I never thought you'd let someone..." Her mother's voice turned tearful and she closed her eyes before whispering. "I just don't know what else to do."

Rosario knew the exact moment her mother was talking about. Even now, the weight of what happened nearly brought her to tears. She could still feel the dirt and tears on her face, could still see the fear clear in her mother's eyes. All she wanted to do was scream and yell, let her mother know it wasn't about letting, it had been about taking.

"Mom, I didn't--I don't--"

"I know, mija, I know...but would you at least go once? Just for me?" Her mother pulled her into a hug and pressed a kiss to her temple. It would be so easy for her to crumble, to break down in her mother's arms. But she couldn't talk about it. She had to protect him, to keep the truth locked down tight.

"I love you, but I can't promise anything." She hugged her mother tightly for another moment before pulling away. She felt the cold air between them like a solid thing pushing distance where there shouldn't have been any. Her mother sighed softly and turned back to the laundry. She measured out detergent, slammed the door shut, and wiggled a few nobs around before the washer stuttered into working. The machines were old and worn, just like this house, but they still got the job done, so her mother kept them around. She scooped up the fresh laundry and, with one last kiss to Rosario's forehead, swept out of the room.

Rosario stayed seated until her mother's footsteps reached the top of the stairs, but as soon as she retreated Rosario was up on her feet, pulling on a rumpled up hoodie that had been thrown haphazardly over the back of the couch. She palmed her keys and made her way out the front door, taking extra care to close the door as silently as possible. She hopped into her car, flinching at the loud noise it made as it started up. She pulled away from the curb quickly, but not quick enough. She saw her mother's head looking out at the street from the top floor and guilt pooled in her stomach.

Rosario drove aimlessly, playing her mother's words over again in her head. She knew that the only reason her mother brought anything up was because she was worried about her. Like most mothers, hers was well intentioned and loving. But that wasn't enough of an inspiration to get her to open up to a stranger about something she couldn't even admit to herself. So instead of thinking and feeling, she decided to drive. All roads here led to the beach, so she soon found herself parking and walking out onto the sand. She stopped at a rock and bent to strip off her shoes and socks. Mid-motion, a hand fell on her shoulder. Rosario startled so hard she nearly toppled over into the sand.

"Whoa!" The hand on her shoulder gripped tighter and kept her from eating it. "I didn't mean to scare you like that." As soon as she was stable the hand pulled away. Rosario turned to come face to face with Michael.

"Oh, Micahel! Uh, hi!" Rosario finished pulling off her socks before standing and dropping them onto the rock. "I'm not usually this jumpy. I promise."

"Uh huh. Sure you're not." Michael grinned and rocked back onto the heels of his Chucks. "What brings you out here tonight?"

"Just...exploring the town."

"Want to take a walk?"

"Yeah, sure." Rosario followed behind him as he made his way to the shoreline. Water lapped at her feet, pulling back before crashing forward once again. They walked in silence for a while, only the sounds of seagulls and calm waves filling the air between them.

"So, Ro. What'd you think of everyone?" Michael asked, his gaze searching the ground.

"Well, to be honest, I'm a little intimidated?" Rosario said, huffing out a breath.

"Don't be." Michael paused his search and seemed to consider her worlds for a moment. "We don't get a lot of fresh blood, so if we came on a little strong it's because we're rusty." Michael glanced up and met her eyes to smile reassuringly before dropping his gaze back to the sand again.

"It's not that. It's just...you guys all seem to know each other really well."

Michael hummed in agreement before crouching down in the sand to sift through some debris. After a few moments he stood, his fingers cupped gently around whatever he picked up.

"I get that." He gestured for her to hold out her hand. She gave him a wary look before sticking out her arm, palm facing up. "But think about it this way—it just means you have us here to look out for you now." He dropped a piece of bright blue-green glass into her hand. It was foggy and soft at the edges, nearly a stone.

"What is this?" Rosario asked.

"Sea glass. It's pollution, really. But the ocean and time take it from garbage to something soft and beautiful. I always liked the symbolism." Michael shrugged and kept walking, eyes scanning the ground for more glass. Rosario smiled and turned the sliver in her hand over a few times before pocketing it and moving to follow Michael further down the beach.

They walked like that for a long time, trading stories back and forth easily, before they reached a point too narrow to pass without going knee deep in the icy water.

Michael looped an arm around her shoulder and moved to turn them around. They walked like that down the beach, feet sinking slightly into the wet sand, until suddenly Michael gave her a sharp shove toward the ocean. Ro shrieked in surprise, nearly falling face first into the slimy cold sand. She managed to stay upright, but in the process ended up further into the ocean. The water lapped at her shins and she was glad she'd had the foresight to take off her shoes.

"What the hell!" Rosario sputtered. She reached out to grab Michael by the wrist and pull him in, but he back-stepped away from her with a laugh.

"Yeah right, like I'm going to let you get me back." He jogged up the beach, away from the water, and waited for her to follow. Rosario let out a frustrated sigh before picking her way around slimy seaweed and up back toward the warm, dry sand.

"I'm going to remember that for next time." Rosario fixed him with a deadly glare, but all it did was make Michael laugh harder.

They made their way back to the parking lot, and Michael tried repeatedly to get Rosario to laugh, while Ro did her best to remain stone-faced. He wasn't going to get off the hook that easily. By the time she made it back to her car, shoes in hand, she'd broken down and laughed at one of the stories he was telling about a time he and Paul had tried to plan a cross country road trip, but hadn't even made it past county lines.

"Paul had the excellent idea to route us through all of the most 'scenic' spots along the way. We couldn't even find the first one on the list. And it was so remote we didn't have any cell service. Paul got so lost it took us basically the whole day to find our way back home."

Rosario drove home with a smile on her face. When she got back inside, her mother didn't ask when she'd gone. Rosario wanted to say *I know you're just worried. I'm worried too. We'll be alright together. All we need is each other.* But instead of saying any of that, she sat down beside her mom and started folding towels, their hands working in sync.

Rosario knew she was dreaming. But dreaming wasn't really the right word for it. She was remembering, feeling it all again, and it was filling her with dread.

She walked toward the door, its familiar white paint peeling at the edges. She pressed her ear to the door and heard whispers, then silence. It stretched on for so long that when she gently pushed open the door it's quiet hinges screamed in protest.

On the bed there was a girl, and she was beautiful. Her long tan legs were intertwined with his, her chest heaving, her head arched to the side. His arms were wrapped around her slim shoulders, his head burrowed into the spot where her neck met her shoulders. He was brushing the area with kisses.

Rosario gripped the door frame and fought to keep from vomiting.

The girl opened her eyes and for a moment Rosario panicked, feeling as if she'd been caught. As if she was the one to be ashamed of her actions. For a beat their eyes held one another before the girl tipped her head back and laughed.

She expected his body to go rigid, for him to feel ashamed, but he didn't even pause his actions. He kept kissing along her skin even as he moved to sit up. He dropped his lips to hers and Rosario couldn't even blink, eyes burning with tears.

Then he stood and walked over to where Rosario was frozen. He cupped her face in his hands and used his thumbs to wipe away the tears that had slipped free and spilled down her cheeks.

"Sshhh, it's okay." He leaned down to kiss her forehead and she shuddered, knowing where those lips had just been. He pulled back and lifted her head up, forcing her to meet his eyes. They were soft, concerned, and full of love. "You know why this happened, don't you?" Cold dread pooled low in her stomach, mixing awfully with the nausea there. She choked out a sob and nodded. His eyes shut as if he was in pain before he opened them again and gave her a hard look. "It didn't have to be this way. I never wanted this to happen. I love you so much, Rosie. All I ever wanted to do was show you how much I love you."

"I love you too," Rosario whispered brokenly.

"Then why won't you let me show it?" His grip on her face turned painful, bruising, but she welcomed it. Anything to distract her from the swirl of emotions storming through her chest. "Why won't you love back? All I've ever wanted to do is show you how much I love you. Show everyone how much I love you."

If you love me, then why did you do this? she thought. If you loved me, you wouldn't do this.

"I'm sorry..." Rosario whispered. "I hate feeling this way. Seeing this...I don't ever want to feel this way again."

"Now you know how I feel when you walk all over my love for you," he whispered fiercely, finally releasing her face. Blood rushed back to her head painfully. "Now will you let me love you?"

"I can't..." she whispered brokenly. "You know I can't..." His open, tender eyes suddenly flickered to life with anger seething in their depths.

"Then just LEAVE!" He grabbed her tightly by the shoulder and pushed her against the wall. "Get out and don't come back until you're done fucking with my heart." He yanked her back up before slamming her up against the paint again. Her head cracked against the wall and her vision swam. She was shaking, her knees weak, but she did her best to push herself back and move on. She'd only made it a few steps before he came up behind her and wrapped her arms around her middle tenderly. "I'm so sorry," he whispered into the crown of her hair. "You just make me crazy sometimes. You know that, right?"

"I know," she murmured. "I'm sorry."

"It's okay, baby." He kissed the top of her head and squeezed her gently. "We'll figure this out together. I'll love you forever, no matter what."

She nodded gently and melted into his embrace.

He'd love her forever. No matter what.

CHAPTER THREE

"Thunder Thighs" -- Miss Eaves

The day of the hike dawned bright and beautiful. Taylor parked outside and waited for Rosario to finish rounding up her things before they could head up the side of the hills toward where they would meet the others. While Taylor idled, Rosario fought to get her long, coarse hair into a bun. She needed to sweep her hair from her face and off of her neck if she was going to get through today. Ever since she was a child, she'd pulled her hair away from her face to focus, and getting through today without embarrassing herself in front of the hottest guy she had seen in a long time meant she would need to focus.

"Ay, mija, come here." Her mother stood outside of the tiny bathroom with a paddle brush and a hair tie already ready to go. Rosario blushed and dropped her hands to her sides. Her mother crowded behind her and brushed out her hair one more time, slowly going from the ends up. She'd always had a tender head, her mother thought it was because her hair was so heavy. The soft sound of a brush making its way in long swipes down her hair helped ebb away her anxiety. Her mother hummed a soft lullaby that she had sung all of her children while she divided Rosario's hair into three even sections. Back and forth she weaved them, creating a thick braid straight down the middle of her back.

"That'll hold better than a bun," she said.

"Gracias madre." Rosario met her mother's eyes in the mirror and smiled. Her mother kissed her on the top of her head before she let Ro past. Rosario scooped up her backpack. She was equipped with a water bottle and granola bars, along with her wallet and house keys. With a quick goodbye over her shoulder, she sprinted from the house and out to Taylor's car.

"You look cute!" Taylor exclaimed as Rosario slid into her front seat.

"Thanks," Rosario blushed. "My mom did it for me."

"And that makes it even cuter." Taylor winked and pulled away from the curb. She blasted 2NE1, a girl Korean pop group Rosario had shared with her earlier in the week. The thought that Taylor liked it made her smile. Rosario hummed along as they made their way through wide city streets all the way down toward narrow mountain roads. Taylor pulled into a dusty and narrow turn off and crept down to a clearing where a bunch of cars were parked. There stood Paul, Kathryn, Scott and Michael under the shade of a huge tree, laughing with one another. Taylor parked close to another car and got out, but Rosario was trapped. She flushed, embarrassed suddenly of her size. She needed just another inch of room, but if she moved the car door at all she'd risk hitting—

"Just open the door all the way." Michael said with a gentle knock to the top of the car. He stooped down, his gaze assessing the situation.

"But then I'll hit the car." Rosario felt herself flush. This was the last thing she needed. Suddenly she felt inadequate in comparison to Kathryn's natural slim figure and Taylor's athletic muscle tone.

"Don't worry, my car can take it." Michael smiled at her and, upon studying her face, continued. "Here, let me hold the door. I'll make sure it doesn't hit anything. Just focus on getting unstuck, alright?"

Rosario nodded, eager to get out of this humiliating situation. Sweat prickled at the back of her neck and she was grateful for the braid keeping her hair from heating up her face even more. Michael opened the door a little bit more, holding it firm as Rosario pushed the last little bit. She quickly stepped aside and Michael closed the passenger side after her. She sighed audibly and looked up at him, bracing herself for laughter, but none came.

"Come on," He grabbed her hand and led her to the others. Paul raised an eyebrow at their linked hands. Michael rolled his eyes and let go of Rosario. Instantly, she missed the tender warmth and couldn't quiet the voice inside of her that wondered if he was ashamed to hold her hand. She shook her head. They weren't anything to each other, so what if he didn't want to hold her hand? That wasn't weird. It was okay. They were okay.

Stop freaking out about not holding hands! she screamed internally.

"Are we ready to go?" Kathryn asked. A murmur of agreement went up before they all began towards the start of the trail, Taylor leading the way. Michael ambled close behind her with Kathryn by his side, then Scott and Paul on either side of Rosario. The trail was wide and well traveled, and the sun was bright but didn't beat down. The cool shade of the surrounding trees contrasted the heat in the air. Rosario walked on quietly, content to listen to the banter while she took in the large groups of trees and brush around her. After about an hour their voices took on more hushed tones until—

"There, can you hear it?" Michael turned around from the front of the group and smiled directly at Rosario. She blinked in confusion before it hit her.

"Oh! The waterfall?"

"Yup!" He grinned and took off with a new energy. In an unspoken unison they all began to dash up the trail. After a few minutes they reached a pool of water with a small waterfall around it. The greenery around it encased them, dense but pristine. A clear path cut through the brush to the waterfall, but all of her friends dropped their bags where they stood, stooping down to remove their shoes and socks. Ro hung back to watch them.

"Gonna join in?" Michael asked as he came to stand at her side.

"I don't know," Ro bit her lip and sighed, overcome with shyness. She always seemed to feel self-conscious at the worst possible moment.

"Come on, we can do it together." Michael grinned. She sat down in the soft grass to remove her shoes and Michael followed. Feet bare they stepped up between Scott and Taylor in the clear cool water.

"Whoa, what do we have here?" Scott yelled. Kathryn shushed him from the other side of the pool. "Michael, *you're putting your feet into the water.*" Scott continued. Rosario turned to look at Michael, who was blushing just a bit at the top of his cheeks.

"Michael is usually a total germaphobe, he always makes up a reason not to go in the ocean with us, and this is like, just as dirty," Taylor chimed in.

Kathryn added with a knowing side eye. "What's gotten into you, Mikey?"

"Shut up," He laughed, the blush spreading down to his neck, "and never call me that again."

All around him the group broke out in the peels of laughter. Rosario was confused, but a glowing sense of happiness bloomed inside her chest nonetheless.

———

Freshman orientation started on the hottest week of the summer. It was the tail end of August, and the ocean air seemed to soak up the heat. Even the morning mist seemed hotter. Rosario drove up with her mother early in the morning to be one of the first to move into her dorm, but even still they were stuck in a line to get her dorm assignment.

Even though Rosario now lived in town, her mother was adamant that she get a dorm and stay on campus for at least one year. The school technically required it, but Rosario heard that they waived the requirement for students who already lived in Coast Village. Her mother said she wanted Ro to have the full college experience, and now she was standing in the middle of a grassy lawn, sweat pricking the back of her ears as she waited for her room assignment.

"Hello there! Welcome to Mount St. Mary's!" said the chipper girl at the table in front of her. Her bright blue t-shirt declared that she was an "Orientation Volunteer" and her hand-lettered name tag announced her as Jessica.

"Thanks," Rosario replied, and put on her most welcoming smile. She wanted to be as positive and outgoing as possible before her inner introvert took over and made her seek quiet once again. All she had to do was get through the day.

"Alright, your name is...?"

"Rosario. Gonzales."

"Okay, I found you!" Jessica said with a smile. "Here's your dorm assignment, and here's a map of the campus." She circled some spots before handing it over. "The circle in red is your dorm, the blue one is the cafeteria, and the green one is the gym. That's where the rest of your orientation is gonna be."

"Wow." Rosario blinked down at the paper, trying to commit their locations to memory. She didn't want to be the one person stumbling around clutching an orientation document, but she had to admit she was a little bit overwhelmed.

"Come on, mija," her mother called from behind her. "Let's go check out your dorm."

Jessica passed them a lanyard with some keys and waved them on. Rosario walked with her mother along a path that was marked every so often by cheerful signs and balloons indicating you were on the right path to reach either the Emerson, Keats, or Thoreau residence halls. The paths eventually branched off, and Rosario followed the road toward Emerson Hall. It was a three story building, housing girls in the first and third floors with boys sandwiched in the middle.

"I bet they love that," Rosario's mother remarked.

"Mad-re!" Rosario exclaimed, lightly slapping her mother on the arm. "You can't just say things like that." Her mother shook her head and laughed.

Emerson Hall was one of the older buildings on campus, the facade faded from time and posters on the wall advertised dances and rallies long since past, but the student lounge was filled with bookshelves and overstuffed chairs, so Rosario was optimistic that she would grow to love it. More people in bright blue shirts buzzed around, helping families find their way around.

"I'm going to go pull the car around," Rosario's mother said. "Why don't you go up and find your room? I'll text you when I park and we can carry your boxes upstairs."

"Aww, what? I have to help?" Rosario groaned. Her mother rolled her eyes and wrapped an arm around her shoulder, moving her toward the stairs. "Fine, fine. I'm going." Rosario reached over to hug her mother before parting ways and darting up the stairs.

Her room was on the third floor, and the stairs were going to be the death of her. Not only because she was gasping for breath at the top of them, but also because she had a knack for falling over. The fact that she managed to stay upright for the entirety of the hike the other day was a miracle in itself. In just the span of three flights of stairs, she stumbled twice. Her shin throbbed where she hit the concrete steps. There would be a nice, purple bruise there soon enough. She rubbed the tender spot and swore from now on she'd take the elevator.

Rosario's dorm room was the first one next to the stairwells. She couldn't tell if the benefit of a quick escape was outweighed by the possibility of loud foot traffic at all hours. With a sigh, she went to put her key in the knob, only to find the door already open. There was a piece of tape over the part of the handle where it locked.

She pushed the door in and took in her new room. It was narrow and dark, with white painted concrete walls and a lofted bed on either side with a desk crammed underneath. There was a small sliver of walkway between the beds. Rosario looked to either side of the door to find a small shoe box closet on either end with a small dresser shoved inside. The right side of the room has several boxes stacked up under the lofted bed and a set of sheets piled up on the mattress. Part of Rosario was sad that she missed the arrival of her roommate, but mostly she was glad there won't be any confrontation on picking sides. It was probably nothing like the movies, but she'd still count it a success if she could make it through the year without pulling that sitcom stunt of drawing a line down the middle of the room in permanent marker, not that black sharpie would show up on this dense grey carpet.

"Hello?" a voice called from over Rosario's shoulder. She flinched at the nearness of the voice and turned quickly. A tiny girl stood in front of her—she couldn't have been much over five feet with pale skin, gauges in her ears, and long bright pink hair with a shaved side.

"Uh, hi!" Rosario smiled and stepped out of the doorway further into the room. "Are you my roommate?"

"Depends." The girl gave her a serious look. "Is this your room?"

"Oh, uh, yeah," she laughed and stuck out her hand. "My name is Rosario, but everyone calls me Ro."

"I'm not going to shake your hand." Blue eyes looked her up and down. "I'm going to hug you!" In a flash, she had strong arms squeezed around Rosario's middle

"Oh, wow," she choked out, her arms coming up to pat lightly on the girl's back. After a moment she let go and stepped away, a bright smile on her face.

"My name's Penelope, by the way." She gestured to her bed. "I hope you don't mind that I picked already."

"No worries," Rosario said. Penelope turned around and fixed her with another assessing look.

"This isn't going to work out."

"Excuse me?" Rosario squeaked. Penelope's gaze betrayed nothing and How had she managed to screw things up already?

"These beds. They're not going to work out. Do you know how hard they are to get into when you're short like us?" Penelope walked up to the side of the bed and stretched up to grab the top railing. She stepped up onto the side of her desk and then jumped, pulling herself half-way onto the bed before wiggling the rest of the way onto the mattress. Rosario couldn't disguise her snort. "See?! You have to admit they're ridiculous!" Penelope sat up and swung her feet off the side.

"On the plus side, you're not going to hit your head on the ceiling," Rosario said.

"Always one to look on the bright side, I see," Penelope snarked. "Well, good luck getting up there, shorty."

"Maybe I'll lower my bed and move the desk next to the closet."

"You might be onto something there, Rosie," Penelope said, and shimmied off the top bunk.

"It's Ro," she responded. Her phone buzzed in her pocket. She woke the screen up to see a text from her mother. "My mom's downstairs with my stuff. I'll be back in a bit."

"OOH, your mom is here?" Penelope perked up. "If I help bring your stuff in, do you think she'll take us to lunch?"

Rosario gave her a funny look and laughed. "She'd probably take you to lunch anyway, but yeah, moving things'll help your chances."

"Awesome." Without missing a beat, Penelope swept her hair up into a side ponytail and marched out the door.

Between the three of them unpacking and organizing, the whole room only took a couple of hours. Penelope got along perfectly with Rosario's mother. Or, as Penelope knew her, "Please, just call me Flora."

Together they took down and rearranged the beds. The new configuration was cramped, but much more livable than vaulting up a desk every time she wanted to take a nap. Her mother helped them both hang up full closets of clothes and put the sheets on their beds. At the end, she did offer to take Penelope out to lunch with them, and Penelope went after a (practiced) demur that she didn't want to intrude was dismissed out of hand. They made their way down through the maze of people and cars out to where Rosario's mother parked the family Tahoe. It was a big midnight blue beast that had seen them through band practice, moves, and more than its fair share of family road trips. Inside, it was a little stained and beaten up, but Penelope didn't blink, just hopped up into the passenger seat.

"Jeez, way to make me take the back," Rosario complained playfully.

"Aye, mija, be a good host!" her mother admonished.

"Yeah, mija, be a good host!" Penelope echoed, turning in her seat to smirk back at Rosario. She rolled her eyes and buckled in, a smile bright on her face.

CHAPTER FOUR

It Had to be You -- Motion City Soundtrack

The evening of Rosario's eighteenth birthday found her sitting alone in her dorm. It was a Saturday night. Penelope was out at some freshman party event, but Rosario hadn't felt like going. She didn't want to spend the night before her birthday feeling melancholy and lonely, so she turned her phone end over end as she paced the small strip of open floor in her room. Michael had given her his number, so texting him wasn't that crazy, right? And if he didn't want to talk to her, he could just not talk to her and it wouldn't be the end of the world. Unless he hated her and decided she was being weird and clingy and—

Her phone buzzed in her hand.

The sensation startled her so much that she let it drop to the ground. It bounced twice before sliding under her desk.

"Dammit," she muttered under her breath. She stuck her arm under the dresser and stretched as far as she could, her fingertips brushing the edge of her phone case. She let out a frustrated sigh and got up, grabbed a hanger from her closet, and laid down to try again. This time, she scooped the phone toward her. It stopped vibrating right as she picked it up. She sighed and wiped the dust from the screen. It lit up and showed a missed call and voicemail from Michael. Rosario grinned so hard her cheeks hurt and unlocked the phone to play the voicemail.

Hey Ro! It's me, Michael. I know classes start up tomorrow so I thought I'd see how you're doing, but you're probably busy. There was some shuffling and mutters and then, *Anyway, that doesn't matter. Sorry to bug you. I just...I hope you're having a good night.*

Rosario smiled and dusted off the phone before tapping out a reply.

Rosario: Got your voicemail. Thanks for calling :) Things are alright.

She hit send and immediately felt self-conscious. But he had called her first, so this was totally okay. Nothing weird about this at all. The phone buzzed in her hand again and relief instantly flooded her tense muscles.

Michael: Just alright?

Rosario: Yeah, just alright.

She paused to consider the tight feeling in her gut before opting for honesty and adding:

Rosario: It's been a weird night.

Michael: Weird how?

Rosario: Weird like it's the night before my birthday and I don't want to spend it making awkward small talk in a room full of strangers.

Rosario stared at the phone for a long while, the 'read' indicator on the message driving her insane. After a few minutes she sighed and turned the ringer on before tossing the phone onto her bed and flopping down next to it. She contemplated just sleeping through all of the troubled feelings in her chest, but she was too restless. Instead she sat up and pulled her laptop off the desk to bring it into her lap. The bottom of the machine warmed the tops of her legs, cozy as she settled in to watch something mindless off of Netflix.

An hour into a horror movie about some kind of monster that she thought might symbolize grief, a knock sounded on the door. She froze, heart thudding in her chest with leftover scary movie adrenaline. Sometime during the movie she had dimmed the lights in the room for ambience, but now as she crept toward the door she questioned her decision. Right as she reached out to open the door, the knock came again. She flinched and gasped.

"Ro?" a familiar voice called from the other side of the metal door. Rosario blinked in confusion before turning on the lights and flinging open the door.

"Michael?" She stared disbelieving at the man standing before her. His hair was windswept, face bright. He was wearing the most ridiculous neon green hoodie, and for some reason that made Rosario laugh out loud. Michael's smile grew at the sound.

"I heard your night was in need of a turn around," he began with a shrug. He had a box under his arm and a small metal keg in his hand.

"Is that...rootbeer?" Rosario asked, pointing at the keg.

"Yeah, well, it's a dry campus, Ro," he teased. "We can't have you getting expelled before classes start."

"I had no idea Ro was such a rebel," Taylor chimed in from behind Michael. Rosario started in surprise, and Michael jumped a bit as well. Taylor shoved past Michael. Further down the hallway stood Paul, Scott, and Kathryn. They waved and went back to talking in low voices to one another.

"Wow Ro, look at this place!" Taylor spun around in the middle of the small walkway between their beds. "You guys got set up quick."

Rosario looked around the room, trying to imagine how Taylor saw it. Their beds were made. Penelope had a floppy stuffed bear seated primly on her pillow with a giant Star-Wars poster looming over it. Rosario's side of the room was a bit more subdued. Her bed was a bit mussed up from where she had been laying, her laptop still open on the bed. An array of polaroid pictures were stuck to the wall by her bed, taken by her little camera that sat in a place of honor on her desk. Beyond that, the only touch they had added to their room was a string of small fairy lights around the window.

"I guess," Rosario shrugged and dropped her gaze back to Taylor's impressed face. "My mom helped out a lot."

"We would have come to help, but it was probably enough of a circus without all of us around too," Michael said as he placed the baby keg down onto Penelope's desk.

"It kind of was a circus." Rosario said. "What are you guys doing here?"

"Call it an early birthday present," Scott chimed in from the hallway, waving a stack of paper cups in the air to be seen over Michael's frame.

"You told them about my birthday?" Rosario couldn't bring herself to be embarrassed, she was just too happy to see all her new friends again.

"In my defense, Facebook would have told them anyway." He gave her a sheepish smile, the harsh overhead lights highlighting the slight blush on his cheeks.

"So can we come in?" Kathryn called from the hallway.

"Oh, right! Sorry, uh, it's a little bit small."

"It's a dorm; we understand," Taylor clapped her on the shoulder before sitting down and scooting up to the very corner of the bed. She patted the seat next to her and looked at Rosario expectantly. After a few moments of shuffling around everyone settled in on the floor.

"Alright, so, I vote we order a pizza," Kathryn said.

"Do pizza places deliver to dorms?" Rosario asked.

"Oh sweetie," Taylor wrapped an arm around her shoulders and pulled her close to her side. "Of course they do. College students live on pizza." Rosario rolled her eyes and smiled.

"Everyone alright with pepperoni?" Paul asked as he pulled out his phone and tapped on the screen. The group murmured their approval before Paul nodded. "Venmo, cash app, bitcoin. Whatever it is you guys better be ready to pay up."

Rosario moved to grab her phone out of her pocket when Michael cut her off.

"Don't worry about it, Ro. I've got your share."

"You don't have to do that, really—"

"No seriously, it's fine," Michael tapped away on his phone. "Besides, it's too late now." He tapped one final button to send his payment through.

"I'm getting the next one," Rosario grinned, pleased that he'd do something nice for her. She still couldn't quite believe that he'd brought everyone together just because she'd mentioned off-handedly that it was going to be her birthday. A few hours ago she'd been melancholy and alone, and now her mood was buoyed up by the people around her and their happy chatter. She sunk easily into the conversation—something about the latest happenings at Michael's band's rehearsal.

Paul unearthed her bluetooth speaker and they started streaming music from a playlist they all added songs to randomly. The mix was jarring—Kathryn's Adele, Michael's Brand New, Paul's twenty one pilots, Scott's Led Zeppelin, Rosario's Motion City Soundtrack, and Taylor's signature Kesha dance track.

The music filled the silence as they scarfed down slices of pizza from a small local mom and pop place that Michael insisted was a campus institution. They didn't have any plates, so Rosario stole paper towels from the bathroom down the hall and they ate with those instead. It was kind of a mess, but everyone was happy enough that they didn't seem to mind too much. Rosario's mother always made dinner a big affair—table set with tablecloth, placemats, and napkins even for the most basic Tuesday night dinner—so having her new friends eat together in less than perfect circumstances gave her a weird feeling of inadequacy. Rosario ate one slice and stopped to watch and see if anyone else went for seconds. To top off her lets-all-eat-off-napkins anxiety she also left weird about being the only one going for seconds. Not only did she not pay for the food, but out of the entire group she was the biggest. She didn't want anyone to think—

Rosario shook her head and tried to derail those panicked thoughts. These people, though new to her, had only shown her kindness. They'd gathered up their money and games and drinks and made the trek out to her school on the drop of a dime even though they'd only met her a few weeks ago. Still, Rosario could not stop from worrying that they were judging her, seeing her as something less than. She thought back to that hiking day with a wince. She'd been the slowest, unable to squeeze between the parked cars. Surely they noticed. Even if Michael had—

"Ro? Hello?" Michael nudged her foot with his elbow.

"What?" Rosario asked, blinking away the dew in her eyes.

"We were asking if you'd ever played Apples to Apples," Taylor offered, giving Rosario a strange look.

"I don't even know what that is," Rosario replied. Michael brandished the box he'd brought in earlier.

"Well, you're about to learn."

It turned out Apples to Apples was about words and guesses and making people laugh, all of which were things Rosario could get behind. After clearing away the pizza mess, they dealt out cards and played two whole games before Penelope walked through the door.

"Whoa." She stopped short. "There are a lot of people in here right now."

"Guys, this is Penelope, my roommate." The room broke out into a chorus of hellos. Penelope took it all in stride and gave a friendly wave. "They all kind of came up here and surprised me." Rosario gave Penelope an apologetic smile.

"It's her birthday tomorrow," Scott interjected. "In case she was trying to weasel out of telling you."

"Not everyone needs to know that it's my birthday," Rosario muttered.

"What?! That's awesome! Happy Birthday! In thirty minutes." Penelope stared down at the boys on the floor before they got the message and scooted their feet back, giving Penelope just enough room to tip toe over to Rosario's bed. She reached over and gave Rosario a warm hug.

"In thirty minutes? Really?" Kathryn took her phone out of her pocket to check the time. "Guys, we've been here for a while."

"Yeah, not that you guys don't seem great and all, but we've got classes in the morning," Penelope spoke as she poked through her dresser and pulled out a pair of sleep pants. "Maybe you could move the party out into the common room so that I can get some sleep?"

"We should probably just head out," Scott said. The group murmured their agreement and began rounding up cups and returning cards. Rosario slipped off the bed and pulled on her boots to walk them out to the parking lot. They walked out of the dorm with a round of goodnights to Penelope. Once they were outside, it was eerily quiet. The campus itself was small and built into the side of a green mountain, so the trees insulated them in a canopy of silence. Rows of little lights lined the path back to the parking lot, but Michael stopped and stared at a point where they diverged, causing the group to come to a stop.

"Michael?" Rosario questioned. He gave her a strange, considering gaze before smiling softly and holding out his hand.

"Come on. Follow me."

Rosario placed her hand in his without thinking. His grip was warm, hand softly calloused on the fingertips from playing guitar. He laced his fingers in hers and guided her down a dirt path that drifted away from the lights. The others muttered behind them before their footsteps followed.

At one point their path brought them behind a set of dorms and cafeteria, and finally down past the soccer field, into a small clearing surrounded by large trees. Michael pulled her into the middle of it all before he released her hand.

"What is this place?" she asked. Within the last few minutes, she'd been led through more of the campus than she'd ever seen, but none of it had really stuck. This place seemed decidedly unmonitored by the university. The grass was overgrown and full of little purple weeds, trees were crowning the clearing with branches heavy with flowers.

Instead of answering, Michael laid out on his back in the dry grass. Rosario hesitated, but he offered his hand. She reached out, eager to feel that warmth again. He pulled her down sharply and she let out a yelp, but he braced her shoulders before she flopped down on top of him and placed her softly in the grass a few inches away. Michael met her gaze in the darkness for a moment before tipping his head back and looking up. Rosario mimicked him and lost her breath.

"I used to come here all the time, anytime I got too far in my own head." His voice barely carried over to where Rosario lay, as if he didn't want to break the stillness of the moment.

Rosario had always grown up in the city. Her town had been decidedly un-city like, but it was big and loud and bright, full of tract homes and shopping malls and brightly lit parks. But here, laying in the darkness of something that bordered on being a forest, she saw stars. They swirled above her in the sky, twinkling and shimmering in a way she only thought people spoke about in songs. She couldn't hold back her gasp. Michael turned his head her way and even in the darkness she could sense his smile. They laid like that in the grass for a while, simply staring up at the stars, until—

"Guys, it's cold out here. Can we go now?" Kathryn muttered. Rosario sat up reluctantly to find the rest of her friends standing at the end of the clearing near the path, huddled together in the darkness. Looking at them, Rosario felt herself shivering too. After a moment Michael sat up and gave her a serious look.

"You didn't tell me you were cold," he said to her in a soft tone.

"I didn't think I was," Rosario responded. He stood up and dusted off his pants before offering his hand and pulling her onto her feet. She brushed the grass off the back of her pants when suddenly she felt a warm weight around her shoulders and bright green fabric draped around her. A blush spread up her cheeks as she looked up into Michael's eyes, bright even in the darkness.

"Thanks," she whispered as she slipped on the hoodie.

"No worries." He tugged the hood up over her head before walking back to where their friends were waiting. He led them all back toward the parking lot, the group talking in hushed voices the whole way. Rosario knew she was smiling too wide, but despite it, she couldn't keep her happiness inside or her blush down. When they got to the cars, the group split in two, Kathryn and Michael heading off in one direction while Taylor, Paul, and Scott walked Rosario back to the dorm.

"Happy birthday, Ro," Paul said over his shoulder as he walked away.

"Thanks." Rosario walked back to her room, mind whirring. Her day had taken such a strange turn that she didn't know how to process it all. She stood in front of the darkened door for a moment, considering everything that had happened, before she felt her phone buzz in her pocket. She opened it to find a message from Michael. It was a gif of a cat in a birthday hat in front of a bright pink cake. She blinked in confusion before another text came in.

Michael: Happy birthday! I hope you have more fun than this cat.

Rosario laughed and tapped out a thanks before shoving the phone back into her pocket and heading into her dorm to go to sleep. After she brushed her teeth and washed her face, she checked her phone one more time to find a slew of new texts—one from each of her new friends here—all wishing her a happy birthday.

CHAPTER FIVE

Raising Hell -- Kesha feat. Big Freedia

The first day of classes dawned bright, sunny, and hot.

"Ugh, this air is crazy," Penelope complained as they walked toward the dining hall. She scooped her hair up into a crazy sideways bun as they made their way through the throng of people. "Why is it so humid?"

"It's barely humid; don't be so dramatic," Rosario chided.

"My life is drama, okay?" Penelope sassed with a smile. They took their trays through the small dining area, loading up with cereal, fruit, and coffee before making their way toward a two top table by the windows at the back of the room. Penelope hopped into the high bar stool seat and immediately began shoveling cereal into her mouth.

"Jeez, slow down."

"Dude, we have chapel in like fifteen minutes," Penelope said mid-bite. "We need to hurry up."

"What? That can't be right." Rosario felt her pulse pick up. There was no way she was behind already on her first day.

"Okay, so maybe we have like twenty minutes." Penelope shrugged. "Maybe twenty-five."

"Oh my god. I hate you so much," Rosario sighed with relief and peeled her banana, slicing it into her cereal before beginning to eat.

"You hate me? How about I hate you for eating the devil fruits," Penelope gestured toward the perfect bite of banana and cereal on Rosario's spoon. "Bananas are gross and everyone knows it."

"Please, can we not bicker before I've had coffee?" Rosario smiled around her spoon. "I want us to live in sweet roommate marital bliss."

"Agreed," Penelope said before biting into her slice of cantaloupe. "In fact I propose we have a two coffee prerequisite before all serious conversations."

"Seconded," Rosario responded in mock seriousness.

"And the motion passes!" Penelope banged her spoon on the table like a gavel, causing the people around them to start and cast them dirty looks. They giggled and finished up their meals, content to be together in silence.

They cleared the table and dashed across campus just as the last chapel cards were being handed out. They each managed to grab one and find seats in the back pews where they scribbled their names out on the pieces of paper that they would hand in as they left the service. For an hour they listened to speeches from different faculty about campus rules, upcoming events, and on how to "make the most out of their college experience."

Penelope scrolled through Instagram for most of the presentation, but Rosario was happy to take it all in. She would be jaded in a few weeks, using this time to frantically finish up homework, but for now she enjoyed it for what it was. When the service ended, the students rushed out in waves, throwing their slips of paper into a bin that would be counted out and totaled toward their yearly chapel requirements. It seemed quaint to Rosario, but Penelope was unimpressed.

"Trust me, I went to a Catholic high school. Chapel every day, not this twice a week set up, but you'll get tired of it all the same."

"I wouldn't have picked a religious school if I had a problem with chapel, unlike some people," Rosario said, casting Penelope a sly smile.

"Oh shut up." Penelope rolled her eyes and shoved her before breaking away and heading toward the other side of campus for her computer science class.

Today Rosario was starting with a Shakespeare class. She'd gone over the plays in high school, so she didn't think there would be many surprises in store for her this semester. She wanted her first few months at college to be easy, so she picked classes she was reasonably comfortable with for her first semester: Shakespearean Comedies, Psychology 101, New Testament, and Sociology. Her mother warned her that she was in for months of long nights full of reading, but Rosario didn't mind. She wanted to get as many general requirements out of the way before she decided on her major.

Rosario picked her way through the open seats toward one in the middle of the class. Oh God, her major. What was she going to do? Penelope had already planned out her entire four years of classes and Rosario still couldn't pick a direction to start. Rosario sighed deeply, took out her notebook and pen, and surveyed the room. There were about twenty other people around her, some talking in groups, but most sitting quietly just like her. She tapped her pen to her notebook and briefly felt self-conscious for being one of the few who opted for handwritten notes. Almost everyone else in the class had their laptops out. Of those, most were either on tumblr or messaging each other in iMessage. She pulled out her phone to keep busy, only to find another text from Michael.

Michael: How's the birthday going, birthday girl?

Rosario rolled her eyes before responding.

Rosario: Just got out of chapel, about to start Shakespeare. You?

Michael: In a church meeting. B O R E D.

Rosario: Isn't that blasphemy?

Michael: I don't know, you're the one in a Christian school. shouldn't they be teaching you this?

Rosario: Be nice, it's my first day. Also, you can't say anything you graduated from here.

Michael:You got me. Hopefully you pay better attention than I did.

Rosario grinned at her phone and hoped no one noticed.

Michael: Hey who do you have for Shakespeare?

Before Rosario could respond, a man walked into the room and closed the door sharply behind him. Rosario's head shot up and she slid her phone into her pocket on reflex.

"Hello class, I'm Dr. Randal, but you can just call me Vince." The man at the front of the room stood tall with wire rim glasses perched at the end of his hawkish nose, shaggy grey hair leading toward a perfectly groomed salt and pepper beard. He was in a cozy looking sweater that made Rosario sweat by looking at it. He placed his brown leather satchel on the desk before pulling out a stack of papers he began to hand out to the class. He spoke for a while about class procedure, guided them through the syllabus, and finally made each student stand up and say something about themselves. Rosario always hated this part of starting school. It seemed a bit childish to do it in college, but regardless she still stood and said her favorite color (blue) and the best thing she'd ever eaten (breakfast taco from a food truck in Austin). They moved through a litany of faces, but at the end of it all, it was too much of a blur for her to remember anyone's name. At the end of the hour, Dr. Randal ushered them out the door with a smile, and Rosario's chest tightened. One class down, one semester full of classes to go.

"Mija! How is your first day of classes going?" Her mother's voice came through the speakers of her phone distorted.

"Mama, I think you need to stop doing whatever it is you're doing." There was a bit of banging, and then—

"Is that better?"

"Much." Rosario sighed. "What were you even doing anyway?"

"Nothing." Rosario's mother said hurriedly. "Anyway, mija, I want to pick you up for a birthday dinner."

"Aw, mom, no, c'mon—"

"Please mija, just do this for me." Her mother used a voice that she couldn't resist.

"Fine. Okay. I'll go." Rosario rolled her eyes and smiled, secretly pleased that her mother wanted to do something for her.

"Good. I'll be there to pick you up at five."

"Mama, it's almost four now."

"Ay, mija! Is it?" Her mother dropped something with a clatter. "Never mind. Five sharp, meet me out in the parking lot by the front of your dorm. I mean it, mija, don't be late!"

"Yes, madre. I love you." She hung up and sighed, knowing her mother would be the one that was late. Regardless she found herself waiting outside of the dorm right on time, waiting in the cooling air for a ride. The heat of the day was beginning to mellow out and she was under the shade of a particularly densely leaved tree. For a moment she closed her eyes and breathed in deep, tasting the air that was different here than anywhere else, before a sharp honk knocked her out of her reverie.

"Ro! C'mon!" Taylor was half hanging out of the window of her beetle.

"Taylor?" Rosario called as she walked up to the car. "What are you doing here?"

"Your mom sent me to come pick you up." Taylor grinned and unlocked the door. "Now let's go." Rosario slid into her seat and gave her friend a dubious look, which only served to make Taylor laugh. "Don't give me that glare, it's your birthday! Be happy!"

"I feel like I'm going to regret this..." Rosario muttered. Taylor smiled and switched on her radio, pulling up that same playlist her friends had put together the night before. A Troye Sevian song came on with lyrics that made Rosario's chest feel tight. She flipped out her phone and scrolled through her notifications, knocking them off one by one, glancing up every now and then as the scenery rolled by.

After a while Taylor pulled down an unfamiliar road that boarded on the sandy beach before pulling into a crowded parking lot. Rosario blinked up at her in confusion.

"C'mon, follow me." Taylor beckoned her friend to follow. Rosario got up out of the car and let her door fall shut as she scanned the nearby tables to find her mother laying out dish after dish. A wave of love washed over her at the sight, her earlier complaining about the dinner completely forgotten. She hurried to follow Taylor out toward the sand.

"Madre!" Rosario called, coming to stand beside her mother and wrap her in a tight hug. Her mother held her close and ran soft fingers through her hair. Tears burned at the end of her vision. After a long day of working a new job Rosario's mother had taken the time to put together a whole surprise dinner at the beach for her. Instantly she felt ungrateful for her tone earlier, but as she pulled back to apologize she was met by her mother's understanding eyes and instead she just smiled. "Gracias, madre."

"Anything for you my darling girl." Her mother cupped her face in her hands and kissed her on the forehead. Then she straightened up and said, a bit louder, "But that's no way to act in front of your friends!" Rosario blinked and looked over her shoulder to find three familiar faces.

"What?!" In front of her stood Peter, Wade, and Kamala, her three closest friends from back home. "How...I mean...what?"

"Look, she doesn't even know how to process this!" Wade threw his head back and laughed. Peter punched him in the arm before jogging up to Rosario's side and wrapping her in a tight hug.

"Happy birthday, birthday girl!" Kamala called out before jumping onto the hug, squeezing the two of them in even tighter.

"Oh man, here we go!" Wade yelled before running at them, hugging them and tackling them all to the ground. They landed in a heap of elbows and laughter.

"I feel like we're missing out here."

Rosario looked up from beneath Wade's arm to find Michael standing over them, a wry smile on his face. Rosario blushed and tried to stand, only to get taken back down by a deft twist of Peter's leg. Michael laughed and offered out his hand which Rosario took gratefully. He pulled her gently from the group on the ground and brought her to stand by his side.

"Michael, these are my friends from back home. Wade, Peter, and Kamala." They all waved as they were mentioned before they worked their way into standing. "But I have no idea what they're doing here."

"We weren't going to miss your birthday for the first time in six years." Kamala said.

"At least, not if we could help it." Peter added.

"I'm just here for the food." Wade shrugged and made his way over to where Rosario's mother was setting up plates and bowls.

"Me too." Taylor called with a wink from where she was standing near Rosario's mother. Rosario could see her brother Israel playing down by the shoreline, his bright orange swim trunks standing out against the dark blue ocean.

"Scott, Paul, and Kathryn are on their way too." Michael added, his voice soft over the sound of the waves.

"Wow...I don't even know what to say." Rosario muttered. She couldn't process all of this—her new friends and old friends all here at once just for this one random day. It was too much, all of it, but she was deeply happy. Michael was standing close enough to her that she could feel his warmth. Without thinking she linked her arm in his and smiled up at him. "Can we go down to the water?" Michael nodded and let himself be led by Rosario down to where Israel was playing. He saw them coming and ran to meet them, chattering loudly about his day so far in his new school. Rosario nodded along and Michael interjected at all the right times, prodding him for more information, before they came to stop just at the point where the waves lapped at the sand. Rosario inched forward, her toes getting splashed softly by the edge of a wave, before she felt Michael stiffen at her side.

"Michael?" She looked up in question. He was looking out at the ocean strangely, his whole body tense.

"It's nothing." He muttered before gently pulling his arm out of hers. "I'm just going to go see if your mom needs any help. Okay?"

Before she could say anything he walked off, leaving her with her little brother who hadn't even stopped long enough to register the change in atmosphere. Rosario couldn't help but feel a little bit disappointed. The cold ocean salt air felt even icier against where his warmth had been. After a few minutes of not responding to him Israel gave up and walked over to the table where everyone was waiting.

"He doesn't like the ocean." Taylor said from Rosario's side. She jumped, unaware of when her friend had joined her.

"Oh...right...I guess you mentioned that, huh?" Rosario gave a small, embarrassed smile.

"Yeah." Taylor wrapped an arm around her shoulders. "I'm kind of surprised he let you drag him down here at all."

"Hey, I didn't drag him," she muttered, a blush spilling across her cheeks.

"Sure you didn't." Taylor laughed. "But somehow he ended up with his toes in the water and another human being in his personal bubble so you tell me what happened."

Rosario's blush deepened.

"Come on, let's eat." She deflected.

Her friends got along just fine together, much to her relief. She didn't know if everyone would know not to take Wade too seriously, but he and Paul got along just fine. And Peter seemed to hit it off great with Scott, so much so that Wade felt he had to kiss Peter right in front of everyone to stake his claim.

"He's been my boyfriend for four years, so you can all back off!" He yelled afterward, Peter's glasses askew over his blushing cheeks. Kathryn laughed so hard she nearly choked on a piece of barbecue chicken.

All in all, it was a rather successful dinner. And as the sky turned from blue, to orange, to pinky darkness their laughter continued to ring out until finally they said their goodbyes under a sky full of barely twinkling stars.

As her mother dropped her back off at campus with a goodbye kiss and a Tupperware full of cake for Penelope. Rosario felt her pocket vibrate. She pulled out her phone as she climbed the stairs—almost tripping in the process.

Michael: Hey, do you still have my hoodie?

Rosario smiled mischievously as she entered her dorm. It was empty, so she quickly pulled on the bright green jacket before snapping a picture of herself and sending it

Rosario: What hoodie?

She smiled to herself and slid off the jacket, hanging it up gently back in her closet. She took her things to the communal bathroom to get ready for bed. When she returned to the room she had three messages. One was a picture from Wade, he was laying in the pull out bed at Rosario's mom's house with Peter and Kamala on either side. He had put a sticker on it that said "GOODNIGHT BIRTHDAY GIRL" in loopy pink writing. Rosario snickered to herself and saved the image before scrolling down to read her thread with Michael.

Michael: Haha, very funny.

And then, several minutes later.

Michael: I think bright green might be your color, because that sure looks good on you.

Rosario blushed hotly and flopped onto her bed, a wide smile spread across her face.

CHAPTER SIX

I Forgot that You Existed -- Taylor Swift

The next few weeks of classes passed in a flowing routine. Ro went to chapel on Tuesday and Thursday and ate breakfast with Penelope. After her sociology class, shehad lunch in the little clearing Michael showed her, and after her evening psychology class, she hit the gym. Then, on Saturday nights, she went over to madre's house for dinner and laundry, and spent the night so that she could enjoy an evening of watching anime and baking with her little brother Israel before going to church with everyone on Sunday.

Sunday quickly became Rosario's favorite day of the week.

It wasn't for the good, God fearing reason. No, it was her favorite because during worship she stood next to her friends while they sang together at the top of their lungs, not caring if she was off key. Kathryn would often catch her eyes and smile, and Rosario would smile brightly back. Michael was always busy with the youth service elsewhere, but even though she missed his presence, church was its own reward.

And maybe it was God somehow in all of it, in the way that they all fit together, and Rosario was happy. She fell in step with her pleasant routine, waking up on Sunday morning to do her hair and dress in her favorite skater skirt and scoop neck navy top. She drove with her mom and Israel, and laughed with all of her friends before the service.

Until the day when she went to church and found him waiting there for her.

The morning had been beautiful--all sun and cool ocean breezes. Michael walked the church grounds with Rosario aimlessly before service.

"I have to say, I'm loving the show but there are SO MANY episodes," Rosario groaned, playing it up to hear Michael laugh. He patted her gently on the shoulder and Rosario could feel the guitar string calluses on her exposed skin.

"If you think that's bad just wait until he gets you to watch One Piece."

"Is that the one with like, over six hundred episodes?"

"Yup," Michael glanced down to note Rosario's horrified face and laughed again. "But they're mostly great! I promise." His footsteps slowed as they approached the youth room. Israel was already inside, watching raptly as a girl on her Switch discussed the strategic use of mushrooms in Mario Kart. Michael looked eager to join in the discussion.

"Alright nerd, I'll talk to you after service." They parted ways and Rosario turned to walk back to the sanctuary, Michael's laughing blue eyes still in the forefront of her memory. She tripped, distracted, and collided head-on with Taylor.

"Whoa, sorry!" Rosario grabbed onto her friend and smiled. "My bad."

"Oh, Ro! Look, we've got another newcomer! Meet Richard."

Rosario took a moment to right herself, as a small blossom of worry grew at the back of her brain. There was no way, it was just a coincidence.

But no. Here *he* was, standing in front of her with his wide white smile, sandy blonde hair combed back neatly and bright brown eyes fixed on her face. He was as handsome as ever, and that felt supremely unfair.

"Oh, Rosie! It's so nice to see you. This is such a surprise!" Richard clapped his large cold hand on her shoulder and she flinched bodily, stepping away from him.

"Uh, Taylor, we actually used to know each other.." Rosario mumbled. The walls inside her quaked at his proximity. She fought to keep her eyes away from him and caught sight of the clumsy kindergarten art on the wall, finger paint and crayon scribbled over outlines of crosses and doves. Rosario tried to focus on the imagery, but anxiety clawed up her throat and kept it closed.

"Hey, Rosie, let's take a walk." Richard said, and turned his trickster face toward Taylor. "Why don't you give us a minute, all right, sweetheart?"

Taylor furrowed her brow in confusion, but before she could say anything, Richard grabbed Rosario by the elbow and steered her toward the front entrance. People were still milling about outside, but he pulled her past them with an iron grip, and she whimpered in pain.

"Give it a rest, won't you?" he hissed as he brought her to the edge of the parking lot. They stood behind the church trailer, blocked off from view. "Stop being so dramatic. That's why I brought you out here to talk. You have no one to pretend for."

"I'm not pretending," Rosario ground out as she wrenched herself free of his grasp. "What the hell are you doing here?"

"Maybe I've had a change of heart. This is a church after all. Isn't everyone supposed to be welcome here?" Richard straightened the long sleeves of his button up. "Maybe I'm on vacation. This place isn't yours alone, you know."

"Get. Out." Rosario managed through gritted teeth, an angry blush heating her cheeks.

"Come on, don't be like that," Richard cooed. "I haven't done anything wrong. I just want to talk to you, let me prove that I've changed."

"I don't want to hear it. Just leave." Rosario said, hating the plea she heard in her voice.

"No, I think I'll stay for the service," Richard said. He kept his tone considering, but Rosario knew he had already planned to stay. Instantly she pictured him on the long drive here from Mooreland plotting how he would get her alone, what he would make her say to take him back. It made a wave of nausea take root in her gut.

He cajoled, "Maybe I'll leave if we can go talk somewhere more private?"

"Not a chance." Rosario glared up at him. He was a good seven inches taller than her, muscular in a way that echoed his time as a wrestler, and he held himself rigid, like she was putting him on edge.

"Then let's go back inside, shall we?" Before Ro could protest, Richard wrapped an arm around her shoulders and led her back inside. His arm was firm around her soft edges, and the contrast reminded her simultaneously of tender moments and unspeakable roughness. Her earlier nausea crested over her in a wave as she fought to not throw up.

The service had already begun. Kathryn was singing up front as Rosario walked in with Richard at her side. Kathryn's voice faltered minutely at the sight of them, but she kept going as if nothing was wrong. And nothing *was* wrong -- not really. As far as anyone knew, they were just friends who had gone to have a talk. Rosario was struck with the realization that no one here knew anything about him. No one except—

"Richard, my mother is here," Rosario whispered. "We have to leave."

"I gave you that option to start with and you turned me down," he replied calmly. "Now we're going to sit here and enjoy the service, won't we?" He glanced down at her with a vicious glint in his eye before fixing his gaze back at the front of the church. Her friends waved at her to come join them in the front pews, but she averted her eyes, horrified at the thought of introducing Richard to them. He was charming when he wanted to be, and she didn't want her friends being tricked by him like she had been.

As the song ended and everyone took a seat, he pulled Ro under his arm and slid her in close. She winced, and as she did, Ro's eyes landed on her mother seated in her normal chair, front and center. Her mother's face was white and ashy, eyes wide. Rosario tried her best to give her mother a reassuring smile, but the service started and they all faced forward to listen to the pastor.

The sermon was on forgiveness, and Rosario hated it. Hated the idea that God would ask her to forgive Richard who still had an arm around her shoulder, hot and an oppressive weight against her. She was sick with the knowledge that he had found her in a place she considered to be safe and happy and full of good memories. But then, about half-way through service, she heard it.

A quiet laugh.

Richard had a hand over his mouth and he was *laughing*. Her horror was so sharp it knocked the breath from her lungs. She elbowed him in the side, but he only laughed louder. A few people seated nearby turned to look at the commotion and Rosario blushed, mortified. These were people she cared for. Dr. Gonzalez, the local pediatrician with a reputation for being ultra stern in her practice but a pushover when it came to babies on baptism day; Tia Beatrice, who wasn't her tia but got along so well with her mother they may as well have been sisters; Mr. and Mrs. Falls, who missed their daughter off at college far from home and often asked Rosario about her plans for the school year—her church family that took care of one another—and here she was sitting with someone who was *laughing* at all of them. Rosario stood suddenly, freeing herself from Richard's grasp, and stormed out of the building. Richard's footsteps echoed as he chased after her. As she made her way toward the exit he grabbed her and pulled her into the courtyard. It wasn't big or spacious, but it allowed natural light to flow into the building and provided a space for the kids to run around after service. Rosario was angry, but she was careful to step around the mini zen garden Israel and his friends had been creating in the dirt.

"Hey, what was that all about?" he asked.

"I can't believe you." Rosario clenched her fist, fingernails biting into her palms. "You were sitting in there *laughing*. Openly mocking something we believe in."

"You have to admit there's a certain humor to it all. You're sitting there talking about spirits and God like kids listening to ghost stories. None of it is real."

"You don't have to believe it, but that doesn't mean you can laugh at us." Rosario moved to go for the door but he stepped in front of her, blocking her exit.

"You didn't always think that," He murmured. "I didn't come here to fight with you, Rosie."

"Then why are you here?" she asked. "You have to know that I don't want to see you."

"Rosie, don't be like that." He reached out to cup her cheek and she leaned into it, muscle memory ingrained into every movement, before freezing and jerking away. It was too late, his mouth was wide and teeth sharp. "I know you still feel something for me."

"Yeah, disgust." She tried to push past him, but this time he grabbed her by the shoulders, his fingers digging into her skin. She tried to shrug him off, but Richard gripped her harder and she bit back a whimper of pain..

"I think we need to sit down and have a little talk, don't you?" He said, the sincerity in his voice so real that she second guessed herself for a moment.

Coast Village was two hours away from Mooreland, and apparently he'd traveled all this way just to see her again, just to find her.

"I promise things are different now. I'm doing a lot better. I just want to talk to you. You were always the only person I wanted to talk about the good things in my life. I always brought the good things to you because I knew you'd be proud of me. I just want you to be proud of me, Rosie."

She considered him, but something in Richard's eyes made her pause.

"No, I don't think I want to do that," she said coldly.

That look in his eyes was too familiar.

"I didn't drive all this way just to get blown off for some ridiculous church service." His voice took on a hard edge. "You're going to come with me."

"I said I don't want to go with you." Rosario repeated, her voice getting louder.

"You act like I'm kidnapping you instead of offering to take you out on a date. You were always ungrateful." His lips twisted into a snarl.

"Let go of me," Rosario insisted, but as she struggled, Richard shook her.

"No, you're coming with me and giving me a chance to *show you*, okay?. If you just *listened* you'd know that—"

"Is there a problem here?"

Rosario froze, that voice familiar, but the tone foreign.

In the doorway stood Michael..

"This is a private conversation." Richard growled, let go of Rosario's shoulder, and put on his best post match interview smile. "If you don't mind, we just need a couple minutes, then we'll be out of your hair."

Michael ignored him.

"Ro, are you all right?" Michael asked.

She met his eyes and felt tears welling up. Where Richard was hard muscle and whitened smiles, Michael was comfy sweaters and messy hair. She longed to reach out to him.

"I'm going to leave now," Rosario stated. The words were for Richard, but her eyes never left Michael's. Richard's hands twitched as if he meant to grab her, but she moved to Michael.

Michael offered his hand. Rosario flinched. Her heart stuttered in her chest, but not for the reason it usually did around Michael. His hand froze in midair before he slowly lowered it back to his side.

"Let me walk you back inside, okay?" Michael murmured.

Rosario fell into step beside him as they made their way back into the service. He left her at the pew next to her mother before walking back out to finish the youth service.

Rosario was too on edge to focus on the sermon, instead she kept replaying Richard's soft tone of voice in contrast to his vice grip on her body. His eyes, full of mean laughter and calculating stares. And his words, begging softly for another chance. She had been so ready to believe him, hopeful that he really had changed when Michael—

Michael. The youth pastor.

Richard had pulled them into the courtyard that was full of windows, surrounded on either side by glass. One of those windows let straight into the room Michael used for Sunday youth service. A hot flush spread through her body at the thought that he had seen their whole conversation. She didn't know what to do with that information, the thought that he had seen someone handle her the way Richard had.

Oh God. Israel had seen that. He had already seen her fall apart so many times over Richard. How many times had he hugged her, his open intuitive heart just knowing when she'd need tenderness after Richard's abuse.

Rosario tipped her head down, her hair falling in a curtain around her, and let silent tears slide down her face. Her face would be puffy and red from crying, but she couldn't stem the flow. Rosario was mortified to find herself crying in a room full of people, but then she felt her mother's soft hand running through her hair. She tensed at the touch initially, but her mother kept up a smooth, gentle, rhythmic motion until Rosario's tears stopped flowing. She sighed and leaned into her mother's side, soothed by the arm that wrapped around her.

When the service ended they made no move to get up as the crowd dispersed. Soon Rosario felt another set of arms wrap around her--Israel, again offering his uncomplicated affection. They sat like that, pressed together, until the church was full of nothing but their soft breaths. Eventually Rosario pulled away and stood on shaky legs. Her mother and brother followed behind her, a hands at the small of her back, and guided her out toward the parking lot. It was empty, only their car around, and Rosario felt the tightness in her chest ease up, finally able to take a full breath.

For now, Richard was gone.

They drove back to the house in silence, not even the radio on to provide something to fill the void. Rosario made it all the way back into the house before her mother spoke.

"Mija, what was he doing here?"

Rosario froze, shoulders bunching up.

"I honestly don't know," she said softly.

"How did he know where to find you?" her mother asked, her concern a blow to the gut. Rosario stared into the walls of the hallway, fixating on the dips of the paint to keep her from tearing up.

"I don't know." she whispered. She'd been so careful this time—changing her number, locking down her social media, untagging herself from posts and pictures. The only people who knew about her new life were people that were close to her. There was no way he should have known. She wracked her brain for how she could have slipped up and came up empty.

Behind her, her mother sighed heavily.

"What's that for?" Rosario asked, on edge.

"Mija, just be honest." Her mother stepped closer, and Rosario tensed with each footfall. Gently her mother reached out to brush back the hair in her face. "Tell me the truth. When did you start talking to him again?"

"I didn't!" Rosario spun around and came face to face with her mother. Where there was usually soft motherly concern were critical sharp edges and a judgmental lift to her brow.

"All I ask is that you be honest with me." Her mother didn't look away, but Rosario broke contact, unable to keep looking at the pain in her mother's eyes. "This is why I think you need to go to therapy."

"Oh my god, seriously?" Rosario threw her hands up and began to walk away.

"This isn't healthy, mija!"

"I know that, madre!" Rosario laughed, nearly hysterical. "Can't you tell I get that now?"

Can't you see how scared I am? she thought to herself, but the words stuck to the back of her throat. She couldn't think of what to say to make her madre believe that this time things were different, that this time she needed to be protected.

It had never stuck before.

On a late summer night, the air was hot and tight,, but a soft breeze brought the scent of baked earth and roasting marshmallows. Rosario had parked her car down the road and was sitting with her headlights off, waiting in the darkness. She took out her phone, the light illuminating the entire inside of her car, and checked her messages.

Richard: Be there in a few minutes. Gotta make sure everyone is asleep.

The timestamp read almost fifty minutes ago and Rosario was starting to get antsy. She contemplated texting back, but she knew if he had left the volume on she'd get in trouble for tipping his grandparents off. She sighed and reclined the seat back all the way, tilting her head back and letting her eyes drift shut while she waited. Her window was cracked, letting in the warm night air and the soft sounds crickets and muted music all around that carried on the wind. The noise lulled her to sleep.

She woke with a start at the sound of a banging door. Rosario jolted up, heart pounding. The first light of dawn slowly illuminated the sky, turning the black night into a barely brighter blue.

When Rosie took out her phone, she found no new messages.. Humiliation welled up inside of her. He hadn't even thought to say anything to her at all, but he knew she'd been out here waiting for him.

Her anger got her out of the car. The air, hot and oppressive that night, had cooled enough to raise goosebumps along her arms.. She crept down the street toward the dingy house at the middle of the cul-de-sac where Richard lived with his grandparents to find the door swinging open noiselessly as she approached, two sets of footsteps making their way down the driveway. . Rosario ducked behind a car parked in the street, breath caught in her throat, and listened to the murmurs. She crouched completely still until the sound passed her by, catching a glimpse of a woman walking away.

The door closed softly and Rosario took that as a cue to get out from hiding. She made her way along the back of the house, getting through the gate soundlessly despite its rusty hinges, before she came to stand at Richard's window. She stood there, silently debating whether or not to go through with it, before the blinds snapped up. Her heart leapt into her chest as his face came into view—furious and beautiful. He disappeared a moment later and she froze, torn between planting her feet in righteous anger or running in fear. Before she could decide, he was slipping out the back door onto the porch.

Richard didn't say anything to her. He yanked her by the arm and drug her toward the shed in the back corner of the yard across unkempt grass. Once they were inside, he shoved her away into a rusty tool table and glared at her from the other side of the dusty enclosure.

"What the hell are you doing here?" he whispered.

Rosario bit her lip and glowered at him. It was hard to explain what was going on without sounding pathetic, she realized.

"Well? Do you just sneak around my house all the time and spy on me? Are you that obsessed with me? God, I swear, you're insane," Richard accused.

"You didn't tell me you weren't going to come meet me," she muttered, a pitiful attempt at avoiding what she wanted to say.

Richard froze, and the anger in his face slipped away, turning into something calculating.

"You waited for me?" he asked.

"I fell asleep," she replied reluctantly.

"Outside, in your car." A smile crept across his face.

"Yes, outside in my car," Rosario hissed, a blush staining her cheeks. She was furious that he was enjoying this.

"That's adorable." He brought her in close to him for a hug.

"No it's not, you jerk," she sighed into the front of his shirt. "Why didn't you say anything to me? I was waiting for you." Somehow, it was easier to talk about it all like this when she didn't have to look at this face. He clasped his hands behind her back and pressed her gently to him.

"I couldn't get away," he murmured, running a soothing hand down her spine. "You know I would have been out to see you if I thought I could."

She didn't say anything in response, simply staying locked in his arms.

He sighed and continued, "Honestly, I thought you had gone home. I didn't know you'd wait there for me."

"I didn't do it on purpose, you know,"she huffed.

"I have a hard time believing you accidentally waited outside my house for five hours." His voice had lightened to something almost truly happy and with it, some of Rosario's hurt eased away. She didn't say anything else, but she relaxed slowly into the hug before she raised her arms up to wrap around him in return. He hummed at the motion and ran his fingers through the end of her ponytail.

"Hey, who was that out there this morning?" asked Ro.

"Hmm?" Richard sounded distracted.

"Someone came out of your door this morning. Who was that?"

Richard's body went rigid beneath her. He wound his hand in her hair and yanked her back. She let out a yelp of pain and struggled to pull away, but his grasp was unyielding.

"So you were sneaking around to spy on me," he hissed, glaring down at her. "That is disgusting, Rosario. What is wrong with you?"

"W-wha?" she asked, still in shock. Her voice was tight with pain. He tugged her hair hard one more time and used his leverage to throw her aside. She stumbled and tripped over the piles of old tools in the shed, falling to her knees.

"Seriously, what I do on my own time is none of your goddamn business," he sneered down at her. "Don't you have better things to do than obsess about every person I see?"

"It was a simple question," Rosario responded, and forced herself to her feet. "But your reaction is making me wonder what exactly I'm missing."

"My reaction? Really? That's priceless. I find you literally camped out in front of my house, trespassing in my backyard, and I'm the one in the wrong."

"You left me waiting! Like an idiot!"

"And you waited, like an idiot!" He quieted, glancing behind the shed door, then answered, "She's a friend of my mom's. God, you're so paranoid. Jesus, can't people come to my house? Are you really that possessive?"

But then why was she leaving so early in the morning? She looked young, even younger than you. If she was just a friend of the family, why are you acting so strange? Rosario bit her lip to keep the words from coming out.

"Okay, okay, I'm sorry," she said. He gave her a calculating look, and she could see him debating whether or not to let this go.

"I mean it," she insisted. "I'm sorry. I know you'd never do anything to hurt me."

"You're right." Richard loomed closer and she took a step back automatically. He went on, "I would never do anything to hurt you."

Richard reached out to caress the side of her face. Rosario leaned into the touch without thinking. Her heart clenched tight in her chest, wondering if his hands had been touching someone else like that this morning.

She mentally shook herself. He said he wouldn't do anything to hurt her. She had to believe that. He leaned down to press a kiss to her forehead and the collar of his shirt slipped.

On his collarbone was a faded but unmistakable smear of lipstick.

"What's wrong?" He pulled away and studied her.

"Nothing," Rosario answered numbly. She fixed her eyes at a point behind his shoulder, a shelf full of old tennis equipment, trying desperately not to peer down his shirt to be sure of what she had seen.

"It's nothing," she repeated.

Richard kissed her lips gently, a hint of minty toothpaste on his breath.

Rosario's heart cracked just a little bit.

CHAPTER SEVEN

Anything for You -- Ludo

Time washed away the harsh edges of most things, there never seemed to be enough time to dull the sting of Ro's memories of Richard. His reappearance shook her to the core, but Rosario kept herself busy, throwing herself into school work and filling all her extra time with taking Israel to the beach with Michael and Taylor, learning how to make tortillas from her madre, and reluctantly beginning to watch One Piece with Michael and Israel.

A late October day dawned bleak and chilly.

"Are you sure you don't want to come?" Penelope asked as she pulled on a bright blue Mt. St. Mary's hoodie. She examined herself in the mirror on the back of their door, adjusting the sideways bun on her head.

"Yeah, I have work to do," Rosario lied. Penelope cast her a glance in the mirror that let Ro know she wasn't fooling anyone.

"I'll bring you back a baby pumpkin," she said, offering Rosario a hopeful look. Rosario tried her best to return the gesture, but even she could see how hollow it looked in the glass. A few minutes later Penelope left with a furrowed brow and cloud of sweet vanilla perfume.

Rosario pulled her laptop onto her bed and queued up an episode of the Office--one with a happy ending--fully prepared to spend the next few hours of alone time trying her best to divert her shouting thoughts. The opening harmonia hums are still playing when a soft tap beckoned from her door. She stood. Her eyes went wide at the sight of Michael standing in the hallway, hair windswept, smile in place, and two coffee cups in his hands.

"Can I come in?" he asked. She blinked up at him for a moment, before stepping aside, happily surprised. Michael ducked inside and put the cups down on her desk.

"What are you doing here?" she asked incredulously. She winced at the sound of the words coming out of her mouth. She was surprised, but she didn't want to sound like she didn't want him here. Simply being around Michael brought her warm feelings and butterflies that she tried hard not to think about too much in his presence.

"I just thought...you know." He shifted his weight around awkwardly before running a hand through his hair. The nervous tic made Michael's hair stand up in an adorable way that made something giddy twitch at the corner of her mouth.

"You just thought..." she gestured for him to continue.

"Sunday was weird," he began, speaking gently to her as though she was a frightened animal he was trying not to spook. "I don't know what happened. And you don't have to tell me. But I," -- he sighed and rubbed the back of his neck -- "I just know this coffee place, Summermoon, just opened up in town and I thought you'd like it so I brought you some. We should go sometime. I mean, I'm sure you and Taylor would love it, they were playing BTS when I left. Anyway, it might get cold soon, though."

Rosario paused for a moment and gave him a considering glance before grabbing one of the cups. Her name was written on the side in a looping scrawl. She passed the other cup to Michael, and as she did, Ro saw a string of numbers printed under his name.

"So did you meet anyone nice at the coffee shop?" she teased. Jealousy pricked the back of her mind, but mostly she wanted to chase the good feeling of having Michael in the same space as her.

"What?" He asked as he brought the cup to his lips and took a sip. Rosario reached out and tapped beside the paper sleeve. He pulled it away from his lips, and as his eyes scanned the writing, his face lit up in a bright red blush. "Uh....I swear I didn't know that was there."

Rosario laughed and tipped her drink back. Immediately, a wash of perfectly brewed coffee spilled over her senses, a slight sweetness to the drink that accentuated the flavor hit her palate.

"This is really good!" she exclaimed. Michael smiled at her before taking a seat on top of her cleared desk. Rosario followed the motion, but on her rumpled bedspread. The wooden frame separated them, but they hovered just close enough that Rosario could smell the spice of his cologne and the chocolate smell of whatever was in his cup.

"What are you drinking?" she asked.

"Hot chocolate."

"No coffee? It's really good, I promise. You want some?" She offered her cup to him, and his face reddened.

"No, I'm all right." He replied, "But you'll never believe what happened at worship band practice." He launched into a tale involving a mouse cozying up in the drum kit. Rosario listened and drank her coffee, happy to have something to take her mind off of the lingering image of Richard in her head.

"You should stop by practice some time," Michael said.

"Me, why?"

"So you could play with us." He gestured to the guitar in the corner of the room.

"Oh, that? I don't know how to play." She tugged at the fabric of her bedsheets self-consciously. "I want to learn though.."

"I could always teach you," he offered.

"Really?" Her heart leapt at the idea.

"Yeah, why not?" He walked over to the instrument and picked it up, strumming and tuning it, before fitting it in his arms and beginning to play a song. It was something sweet. Rosario could tell that much even without words. He moved his lips as if he was mouthing along to a song before softly murmuring a few words.

"My ancestors planted some sequoias down a road, I've driven down that road since I was born…"

Rosario recognized the song as "Anything For You" by the band Ludo and began to hum along. Michael's eyes shot up and his grin grew wide. His voice got louder, singing more exuberantly, before he locked eyes with her and paused. "C'mon Ro, I know you know this one." She rolled her eyes and began to sing along with him.

Together they sang a few songs, Rosario testing his knowledge and Michael throwing melodies her way to see if she could pick them out. Michael belted out cheesy pop ballads with so much gusto that Rosario could easily picture him on stage. His energy encouraged her to sing louder, unashamed of her off key additions, and dance along with him from where she sat. Michael bounced along to the songs, his lanky frame exaggerating every movement, unkempt hair falling into his blue eyes. But most engaging to Rosario was the looks he would throw her way--full of mischief and something she couldn't quite read, but wanted to know intimately. During a particularly romantic Disney song their eyes locked and Rosario felt her heart skip a beat.

"Love is beautiful, love is wonderful, love is everything. Don't you agree? Me oui!" He was singing the song Evangeline from the Princess and the Frog in a false cajun accent, but with his gaze on her she could almost hear something sincere in the song.

Oh no. She thought. *I want this too much.*

They kept up like that—Rosario perched on the edge of the bed, Michael standing in the corner of the room, leaning against the end of the wall, until Penelope came back in with two pumpkins under her arms.

She shook her head, deposited the pumpkins on her bed, and backed out of the dorm without a word.

"Sorry," Michael said, setting down the guitar back in it's dusty corner spot. "I should probably get going…" Rosario bit her lip, unsure for a moment, before responding.

"Let me walk you to your car?"

"Sure," He answered. They made their way out of the dorm and into the brisk night air. They kept up a stream of chatter, Michael pointing out places he used to love, until they reached his car. Michael flipped his keys in his hand a few times before sighing and running the fingers of his free hand through his hair.

"Listen, Ro...about Sunday." He paused and Rosario felt her heart drop.

"We don't have to talk about this," she responded. Michael was looking off into the distance, but at her words he snapped to attention.

"I really think we do," he ran his fingers through his hair again. "I don't need to know everything, but I need to know you're safe. If you ever need me, I'm here. Okay?"

"O-okay…" Rosario felt her voice catch around the lump in her throat. She couldn't even begin to imagine his reaction if she told him about Richard. The things she'd done, the things *he'd* done. "Thanks. I appreciate it."

Michael looked into her eyes, searching, before nodding his head and turning to unlock the car. He had to twist the key back, then forward, then back, then forward quickly to get it to unlock. But he did it smoothly, a ease born of repetition.

His back was facing Rosario, and it might have been the lingering romance of earlier ballads but Rosario felt bold and stepped forward, wrapping her arms around his waist, hugging him from behind. Immediately he tensed and Rosario dropped her arms, prepared to step back. Before she could make a move, Michael's hands reached down to bring her arms back up, pulling them around his torso. It was probably the weirdest hug Rosario had ever given, but she could feel his warmth through the thin fabric of his hoodie and after a moment Micahel entwined his fingers with hers, giving them a soft squeeze before releasing her and turning.

The motion brought them face to face, their height difference making it so Rosario was bumping her nose against his chest. Suddenly she felt a light pressure on the top of her head, but by the time she looked up Michael was looking away. The lighting of the parking lot cast sharp shadows over his face, but Rosario imagined she saw a spill of pink across his cheeks.

"Text me when you get home?" Rosario requested, feeling emboldened by their proximity.

"Sure," he huffed a laugh before stepping away and opening the car door a crack. Rosario took a few steps back to watch as he drove away. Once he was gone she walked back in and flopped down on her bed, a smile on her face, the lingering scent of Michael's cologne still in the air.

"I'm telling you, there's something there," Wade said around a mouthful of chocolate croissant.

"I don't know..." Rosario sat cross-legged on her bed, computer propped up on the desk in front of her. She was munching on a banana and honey sandwich before her morning classes, skyping with Wade and Peter over breakfast. They were sprawled on their couch, sharing a carafe of coffee between them.

"Seriously, I know Wade is usually full of shit, but I think this time he might be onto something." Peter poured himself a fresh cup of steaming coffee and added in a splash of cream, cradling the mug in his hands. "You should ask him out."

"What?!" Rosario choked on her sandwich. "You've got to be kidding me."

"I'm serious!" Peter said. "I bet you he says yes."

"There's no way." Nervous energy buzzed through Rosario.

She hoped -- of course she hoped -- but there was no real proof that he felt what she did when they were together. Plus, she couldn't shake the spectre of Richard. How badly things had gone for her before.

"Fifty bucks says he says yes." Wade gave her a devious lift of his brow.

"I'm not going to ask him out for fifty bucks," Rosario protested.

"Are you sure? Think of all the coffee you could buy with fifty bucks!" Wade responded.

"While that is tempting, I'd rather preserve my fragile ego," Rosario deadpanned.

"Okay okay, let's give her a break," Peter cut in, "But Wade, you have to tell Ro about what happened when we went to my aunt's house last night."

"Oh my God, it was awesome, okay so--"

The conversation carried on after, but thoughts of Michael didn't leave her head. She contributed here and there to the conversation, but her hand was turning the phone over in her palm. The more she thought about it the stronger the urge got to make *something* happen.

"--and that wasn't even including the whipped cream!" Wade cackled.

"I'm going to do it." Rosario said, flipping her phone up into her hand and typing away furiously.

"Do what?" Peter asked at the same moment Wade yelled, "OH MY GOD."

"Is a movie casual enough?" Rosario asked, flipping from bravery to nerves within seconds. Her fingers had typed out a message almost without thinking.

"Whatever you're doing, just hit send!" Wade shouts, lunging toward the camera.

"Wait—" Peter called, shoving Wade out of the way, but it was too late.

Rosario: Hey! Thanks for the coffee the other night. How about I pay you back with a movie? What about that new horror-comedy, I know how much you love Simon Pegg.

"Holy shit," she whispered. The message had been sent. It was sitting, waiting to be read on his phone. A hot blush rushed up her face. She stared at the words for a while, barely blinking. Maybe going with horror was a bit much for a first date. But then, the cuddling possibilities were too tempting to pass up.

"We've got to get to class," Peter said reluctantly. "Has he said anything?"

"Nope." Rosario looked up, her gut churning. "He hasn't even read it. Is it too late to steal his phone and delete the message?"

"That only works in movies," Peter admonished.

"Yeah, this is only book material at best," Wade chimed in.

"Whatever. I'm just going to forget about it." Rosario shoved her phone into the bottom of her backpack before loading it up with her English anthology and a pair of tangled headphones. "Enjoy your classes today boys."

"Let us know when he says yes!" Wade hollered as Peter ended the call.

Rosario sighed and fought to control the adrenaline rushing through her veins. Her knee bounced uncontrollably as she thought over her last few interactions with Micahel.

In class she checked her text messages every few minutes, even though she had sworn she'd wait until she heard the notification sound before checking her phone again. She caught it just in time to see him type, delete, type, delete, and then finally send—

Michael: As long as we're not going alone that should be fine. I know Kathryn and Taylor really wanted to see that movie too.

The blood left Rosario's face as mortification took hold. Quickly she tried to recover.

Rosario: Awesome! I was already going to invite them. Do you think Paul and Scott might want to come too?

He responded to her text almost immediately.

Michael: Probably. Let me check with everyone so we can get a time together.

Rosario thumped her head against her desk and sighed heavily before drafting one more text.

Rosario: Wade, you owe me fifty bucks.

——

The next day was gloomy and rainy and the perfect day for a movie. Rosario huddled beneath her clear umbrella, arriving just as Michael walked up to the ticket counter.

"Don't worry, I've got it," Michael said. Before she could protest, he slid in front of her. "Two please."

The bored-looking attendant took his money and handed two tickets back along with change.

"This was supposed to be me repaying you," she finally managed.

"It's okay. I wanted to do this for you," Michael said with a smile over his shoulder, his eyes crinkling up at the corners.

Rosario stumbled, feeling off kilter with how much this echoed her half-formed wishes of a date between the two of them.

The rest of their group followed them inside.

Taylor grabbed Ro by the arm and looped them together before whispering, "What was that about?"

Rosario shrugged, silently happy she wasn't the only one noticing the interaction. They filed into the theater, Rosario, between Michael and Taylor. She settled into her seat, hyper aware of Michael's warmth beside her. She froze in place, wanting to lean into his warmth but keenly aware of the rejection she'd faced earlier in text. She sat like that through the whole movie, rigid next to his body heat and comforting spicy cologne smell, a weird perversion of the date she had hoped they would have. The movie was good, but Rosario couldn't help but be enraptured by the light on Michael's sharp jawbones and the deep timbre of his laughter. At a particularly spooky part in the movie Michael caught her staring and stuck his tongue out at her, breaking the dark atmosphere and ruining the following jumpscare.

When the lights rose and they stood to leave, Ro sighed an audible breath of relief. Michael looked down at her strangely, and she tried to pass off the noise as nothing.

"Did you like the movie?" he asked, confused.

"Yeah, of course!" She answered, too quick. "I liked the uh..." Had she even been paying attention? What was the plot? Michael quirked an eyebrow at her and she laughed nervously, improvising, "Hey, Taylor, what did you think?"

"I thought it was hilarious, but I am a sucker for practical effects." Rosario focused completely on Taylor, hoping Michael would take the hint and let things drop. He did, though he hopped in to comment on what he had thought of the score, while Rosario nodded with the occasional noise of agreement to seem present. She couldn't get rid of the feeling in her gut that let her know her hopes for this day had been dashed because she misinterpreted things.

Rosario was having a leisurely lunch on campus during her two hour break between classes when a familiar floral skirt bounced into her view.

"Taylor?" Rosario looked up from the book she had been reading and confirmed that yes, Taylor was standing in front of her, dressed in her favorite pink daisy outfit despite the chilly temperatures outside.

"Surprise!" Taylor sat down opposite of her and placed her tray on the table. Rosario had already almost finished eating, but smelling the queso fries on Taylor's plate made her hungry all over again. "I thought I'd come have lunch with you."

"This is the best thing that has happened to me all day," Rosario said as she closed her book and made extra room on the table.

"I know! We haven't gotten to spend one on one time together in so long! Though the movie was fun..." Taylor trailed off and gave Rosario an opportunity to respond, but Ro focused on fidgeting with the wrapper of her straw. "You picked a great movie, Michael loves that kind of stuff."

"I know..." Rosario gathered up her courage and responded, "I was actually trying to make it a date."

"Oh no, why didn't you tell me?" I would have told everyone to cancel or something."

"What?" Rosario blinked. "You don't think I'm out of line?"

"Are you joking?" Taylor asked. "I think you'd be great together. I've been waiting for him to get his act together and ask you out since day one. I bet he was just too dense to even get what you were trying to do."

"I don't know about that," Rosario said. She pulled out her phone to show Taylor the texts.

As Taylor looked them over, a stormy frown took over her face.

"Are you kidding me?" she asked.

"I know." Rosario thumped her head against the table. "I'm so stupid."

"No, he's stupid." She shoved the phone back at Rosario with a disgusted sound. "I swear, I'm going to wail on that kid."

"Please don't say anything!" Rosario shot up in her seat.

"I won't." Taylor nudged Rosario playfully with her elbow. "You can tell me anything. You know that, right? You don't have to keep your crushes from me, even if they're on someone that is basically a brother to me." Taylor stuck out her tongue, pretending to gag.

"Alright," Rosario reached over to pull a cheesy fry from the pile on Taylor's plate, happy that her friend was willing to keep this secret for her. They finished their meal, chatting about their days, before Taylor stilled in her seat and stared toward the entrance of the dining hall.

"What?" Ro asked, following Taylor's line of sight to see a tall, thin woman with braids swooped up into a bun at the top of her head. She was swiping her ID card at the door, a student walking by her side.

"Holy shit, I totally forgot she worked here," Taylor muttered. "That's Michael's ex-girlfriend."

Rosario froze, blood draining from her face, as she took in the woman one more time. She was beautiful. Tall where Rosario was short, thin where Rosario carried soft curves, and stylish in a way that spoke of money Rosario definitely didn't have.

"My competition, huh?" Rosario joked hollowly.

"Don't do that," Taylor gave her a serious look. "Don't compare yourself to her. Besides, she stomped on Michael's heart hard. He was totally blind-sided by what went down. He was miserable for months. Right up until you got here, actually."

"What does she do here?" Rosario asked.

"I think last I heard she was the disability coordinator?" Taylor shrugged. "I'm not really sure."

Rosario heard herself murmur a response, but her mind was completely occupied by the idea of that woman and Michael together. She could clearly picture how they must have been a perfect picture standing arm in arm. Did they go to that secret spot on campus together too? Did he sing her Disney songs about love? Did they kiss goodnight after hugging at the door of his old car?

"What's her name?" Rosario asked.

"Does it matter?" Taylor countered. Rosario tracked her braids through the room, watching as she weaved past rows of round tables and ugly orange chairs. "Her name is Jamara. But stop doing that, alright? I can see you tearing yourself down from here."

"Sorry," Rosario smiled sheepishly, embarrassed that she was so transparent.

"Let's head out of here so you can take your mind off of it, alright?"

Rosario nodded, grabbing her tray as Taylor led them from the room.

The end of the semester pulled Rosario along so hard she barely had time to feel awkward around Michael or even think too much about Richard's reappearance. Rosario's once open weekends turned into late night study sessions in the quiet rooms of the library, groups of peers huddled around open books with empty coffee cups filling up every available surface.

Like clockwork, Taylor appeared on Sunday mornings in a cloud of patterned skirts and Dior perfume outside Rosario's dorm, so she always found a way down to church. Usually her friends could coax her to spend an hour or two having lunch with them, but eventually something snapped.

They're at Michael's apartment, all crammed into his tiny living room with shared plates of Thai food in their laps. Rosario munched on spring rolls while taking in the decor of the room--band setlists were plastered along a wall, an entertainment center held several game consoles and towers of games, and a pile of paperback sci-fi books were placed next to the couch Rosario sat in.

"Alright, I know it's almost finals, but we have to do something fun together," Taylor pleaded over their meal.

"We should do something for Christmas," Kathryn suggested as she reached over Paul's lap and snagged a box half full of pad thai.

"Oh, we should do Friendsmas!" Scott shouted, mouth full of noodles. Michael winced at the sound, and Scott repeated more quietly. "We should do Friendsmas."

Everyone gave him a strange look.

Scott clarified, "Like Christmas, but with your friends?"

"So a Christmas party?" Paul drawled, eyebrow arched.

"Friendsmas party," Scott corrected as he pulled the pad thai box back from Kathryn to find it empty. He frowned and Kathryn stuck her tongue out..

"I love Christmas," Rosario offered, putting down her container of pad see ew. "The lights always make me happy, even if I'm really never sure what to buy." Rosario nursed fond memories of Christmases spent at her abuela's house, tables full of tamales and a tree nearly crowded out of view by piles of presents.

"Well then, you can bet you're going to love Friendsmas just as much," Scott responded

"Yes, I am so excited for Friendsmas!" Taylor wiggled in her seat happily.

"Yes! I told you! Friendsmas!" Scott cheered, pumping his fist in the air.

A chorus of laughter went up at the motion and Rosario forgot all about her growing pile of homework back at her dorm. For now she was with her friends and that was enough.

Two weeks of studying, church Christmas preparation, and wintery mornings passed before the group got together again for their

Friendsmas. They're back at Michael's apartment, Rosario's finals completed but still fresh in her mind.

"Come on, lighten up," Taylor nudged Rosario with her shoulder.

They were sitting next to each other on Michael's hand-me-down couch. It was a bit lumpy and the fabric was worn, but it was comfortable and homey in his house full of garage sale finds and Ikea purchases.

"Sorry," Rosario sighed. "It's just...it's my first semester at college. I want to do well, you know?"

"I get it," Taylor reassured her, "but it's done now. You did the best you could. Now you've just got to wait. And there's no point in making yourself miserable over waiting."

"I guess you're right," Rosario said with another long sigh, "but that's easier said than done."

"How about we take your mind off stuff with the White Elephant?" Taylor offered, loud enough for the whole room to hear.

"We're doing White Elephant now?" Scott asked excitedly from across the room. He had been the one to try and convince everyone to get on board with White Elephant in the first place. Rosario and Taylor giggled at his enthusiasm.

"Yeah, Scott, we can do it now," Taylor dryly said.

"Awesome!" He pumped his fist in the air. "Everyone get in a circle with your presents."

They sat on the floor and passed around presents. Michael ended up with a sparkly WWJD bracelet that he donned immediately, Scott received the itchest scarf in all of creation, and Taylor got a bottle of men's cologne. Rosario was 'fortunate' enough to get a small porcelain doll with a truly terrifying smile stretched across its face. Paul had cackled loudly when she picked it out of the pile and peeled back the wrapping paper.

"I'm definitely donating this. Or selling it on eBay." Rosario said, holding the doll away from her body.

"Yeah, the ad will read: 'for sale: one haunted doll. $0.00 or best offer. free shipping.'" Paul teased. "Give it up, Ro. You're stuck with that thing."

"You're the worst," she groaned as she shoved the doll across the coffee table away from her.

The group got a few laughs in at her expense before devolving into scattered conversations. Michael came up to Rosario's side and beckoned her to follow silently. She heard the faint strains of a heated debate between who's pie was better--Taylor's mom's recipe or Scott's--before the door closed behind them.

The air outside on Michael's porch was just the right side of chilly, enough that Rosario didn't feel exposed in her silly Christmas sweater. Michael rocked back and forth on his feet before running a hand through his hair. After a moment he held out a small package.

"Merry Christmas," he said softly. Michael lifted up her hand and placed the package in her palm. "It's for you. For Christmas."

"Really?" Rosario looked down at the strangely wrapped package in her hand. It looked like Michael had used about seventeen pieces of tape to hold it together, and it was small and light. "Can I open it now?"

Michael nodded.

Rosario tore the wrapping paper off to reveal a set of guitar strings and a package of pearlized guitar picks. There was a note wrapped around it that read: *This coupon is good for guitar lessons. Let's teach you how to rock!*

Rosario glanced up at him in disbelief. "Really?"

"Yeah, of course," he said with a small chuckle. "You look like I just handed you keys to a new car or something."

"I'm just surprised," Rosario said.

"I told you before I'd be happy to teach you," Michael reasoned.

"Yeah, but people say stuff like that all the time." Ro ran her thumb over the note. "Thanks for following through."

"Well, I haven't done anything yet." Michael smiled down at her, cheeks red from the cold. "You can thank me after you know a few chords."

"Right, thanks for nothing," Rosario said with mock seriousness.

Michael tilted his head back and laughed. Rosario brightened at the sound. For a moment she's taken aback by how much she *feels*. Seeing Michael lit up by string lights reminds her of all the ways Michael has been genuine, caring, present. All the things Richard pretended to be but never was. The gap between Rosario and Michael seemed especially small in this quiet moment. Rosario almost stepped back, away from Michael's warmth, but as she did she looked up to see him *so close*. Before she could think too much about it, Rosario closed her eyes and took a deep breath, swimming in the cool air and Michael's cologne.

"Let's get back inside," Michael said breathily, now standing a few feet away. *Had that all been in her head?*

"Sure.." Rosario shook her head to stop it from spinning and followed Michael back inside. Taylor immediately locked eyes with her and waggled her eyebrows, but Rosario only shook her head and huffed a soft laugh, still warm from the private moment she and Michael shared outside. Her gift sat heavy in her pocket. From time to time she brushed her hand against it and a spark of affection blossomed in her chest, finals far from her mind in the midst of the joy that filled the room.

For Christmas Eve, Rosario went back to Mooreland with her family. All of her extended family—from her tias and tios to her baby cousins—lived in the town they had recently left behind. Despite the dark memory of her time in Mooreland with Richard, Rosario was happy to be going back. Her family had always been close, so getting to see everyone else again felt refreshing, like that first jump into a cold pool during the summer.

Her family all went over to her abuela's house for dinner that evening. Rosario had fond memories of stealing eggs from the chicken coops to trade with the neighbor tio Ernesto for Meyer lemons from his tree, and falling asleep on the couch while her abuela watched telenovelas and played with her hair. It all came rushing back the second she stepped foot across the front doorway.

Tamales spilled across the kitchen counter while carne asada sizzled on the grill outside. Tio Ernesto was there, enlisting his grown children in arranging trays over every available inch of room on the antique dining room table.

Rosario ate tamale after tamale--alternating from pork to cheese and jalapeno--and let the conversation flow around her. Her tia Elodia asked about college and everyone was happy for her as they listened to her talk about her classes, but after a while she began to fidget with the sleeve of her hoodie, anxious for the evening to draw to a close. Kamala, Peter and Wade were home for the break as well and Rosario hoped she'd get to see them, but it was getting late.

"Mija, just ask," her mom said as she nudged her with her elbow.

"Hmm?" Rosario asked, distracted by an influx of texts from the group chat she had going with Kamala, Peter and Wade. From what she could tell Wade was currently sending in selfie after selfie and Peter was hyping him up.

"If you want to go see your friends, all you have to do is ask," Her mother intuited.

"Can I go see my friends?" Rosario said timidly. She hated asking for permission, but she knew she would need to borrow her mother's car to go anywhere.

"Of course. Be safe; don't stay out too late. We've got an early morning opening presents with everyone." Her mother patted her hand and placed the keys in Rosario's open palm.

"I know, madre." Rosario kissed her mother on the cheek as she pocketed the keys and walked out of the house. Before she made it far voices rose up behind her.

"Take some lemons!" Tio Ernesto chimed. Rosario doubled back to pick up a few and stuff them in her bag.

"And cookies!" Her abuela added. "You know Kamala loves my hojarascas."

"Aww, I wanted those!" Israel whined.

"I'll leave them for you, you're cuter," Rosario said with a wink. "I love you all, goodbye!"

Deja vu crept down Rosario's spine as she drove to Peter's house. She went through streets she'd been down a million times, but somehow not living here any longer made them feel distant, only familiar. But as soon as she pulled up to Peter's house she was home.

This was where they'd come after school to do homework and play for most of her childhood. These steps were familiar, her feet running up them with muscle memory as she bounded toward the front door. She rang the doorbell and Peter's aunt answered.

"Rosario, come in!" She pulled Rosario into a tight hug that Rosario returned without hesitation.

"Thanks Mae," Rosario stepped inside and wiped her feet on the mat. "Is Peter around?"

"They're all waiting downstairs in the basement." Mae inclined her head toward the door.

Rosario made her way down the steep steps into the wide open basement space. A puffy leather couch dominated the room, but it was dwarfed by the size of the extra large television. At the back of the room a long table crowded a tiny kitchen into a corner. This was where she'd spent most of her after school hours, with her friends eating Aunt Mae's signature spicy popcorn in front of the TV after doing their homework.

"Ro!" Kamala called. "You're just in time. I need to kick their butts in Mario Kart and someone needs to make sure Wade isn't cheating."

"I told you I'll make sure he isn't cheating," Peter said, rolling his eyes.

"I'm sorry, but I can't trust your judgement. You are sleeping with the guy," Kamala smirked and picked up her controller.

"Wow, I can't believe you think so little of me," Peter said, sounding miffed.

"I can. After all, my sexual energy can be quite persuasive," Wade waggled his eyebrows at the group and everyone let out a collective groan.

"All right, I get it now." Peter shoved Wade playfully.

They settled into a few rounds of Mario Kart, Rosario perched on the back of the couch watching the games play out.

"Ah hah! I win AGAIN!" Kamala crowed triumphantly.

"That's it, I need some air," Wade threw down the controller and stood with a huff. Peter pressed a kiss to his cheek and Wade rolled his eyes in exasperation, but his shoulders loosened their tense posture. They pulled on their jackets and shoes before walking back upstairs.

"We're heading out, Aunt Mae," Peter called into the kitchen where Mae was seasoning a cast iron pan.

"Don't stay out too late! You know I can't go to sleep if you're still outside," Aunt Mae answered.

"I'll bring him back soon, don't you worry." Wade said with a grin.

"With you? I always worry," she replied.

Kamala barked out a sharp laugh and Wade shot her a glare.

"Why doesn't anyone think I'm responsible?" he asked, raising his face to the sky as if to direct the question to God himself.

"Because we know you too well," Rosario said, and clapped a hand to his shoulder. "Now let's go."

They all piled into Rosario's mother's car. The SUV could fit them all easily, but Kamala, Peter, and Wade crowded into the same row of seats. Almost on auto-pilot Rosario drove them to the park they had frequented since they were children. It wasn't until she was half way there that dread filled her stomach. Richard often frequented this park too, back when they were dating. He had been able to find her before. Would he find her now? She shook her head and pulled herself back into the moment--she was with her friends. They would keep her safe.

As soon as they arrived, they tumbled out of the car and ran toward the playground equipment. Peter and Wade raced up the jungle gym to slide down the slide together while Kamala made her way to the monkey bars. She swung from rung to rung, laughing the whole time at Peter and Wade's antics as they ran up the slide. Eventually Peter knocked Wade down and showered his face with kisses while Kamala snapped pictures for her Instagram story.

Rosario shook her head and sat down at the swing, slowly pushing herself back and forth.

This park used to only hold memories of her childhood, but after her time with Richard all she could think about was how things used to be.

Last Winter

It was a cold night, especially for California. Rosario had been waiting at the swings for over half an hour before an old pick up truck pulled into the spot next to her mother's SUV. After a moment, the lights cut out and a dark figure unfolded from the driver's seat. She knew that silhouette anywhere.

"Richard," she welcomed, breaking the late night silence.

The lights around the jungle gym shone bright, light cutting through the darkness and illuminated the sharp lines of his face.

"Here." He had two cups in his hands and he held one out to her. "I thought you could use something to warm you up."

Even through the plastic lid she could smell the coffee, and as she took a sip the just right balance of cream, sugar, and coffee exploded across her tongue. Rosario grinned, happy that her boyfriend knew enough about her to know exactly how to mix her favorite drink. They sat in silence for a while before Richard pulled out a cigarette.

Rosario crinkled up her nose as he lit up.

"Still on your high horse about these?" he asked after his first drag.

"They smell, and you know I have asthma." Rosario huffed.

"You'll be fine," He brushed her off, sounding annoyed. "Besides, I'm sure you'd like them if you just stopped being such a baby and gave them a try."

A few moments passed before Richard spoke again.

"Do you love me?"

"What kind of a question is that?" she asked, wary at where this conversation was headed.

"Just answer the question," he insisted.

"Of course I love you," Rosario said, exasperated.

"Then try this for me, just this once."

"I already told you I'm not doing it." Rosario stared defiantly into the distance.

She heard the crunch of gravel under thick soled boots and steeled herself as fingers landed gently on her chin. She went limp, allowing herself to be manhandled, when his lips covered hers.

Automatically she opened for him and smoke filled her mouth.. She breathed in, bringing it down into her lungs, before pulling back and exhaling. Her chest tightened and she jerked back to find Richard smirking down at her.

"Again?" He asked with a grin, waggling his cigarette at her.

Rosario shook her head, feeling slimy dark unease trickle down her spine.

He always got his way, no matter what she said.

She heard the whisper of Richard dragging in before his lips were on hers again.

CHAPTER EIGHT

Blue & Grey -- BTS

Rosario awoke one morning to a gray February day. But as the fog lifted, the gray stayed. The crisp mountain air felt chilling, the blue of the sky muted. There was a film over her day that she could not shake. She had felt this before a few times, coming on slowly when her dad got sick, and slower still each time Richard raised a hand against her. But this time it appeared between one blink and the next. There was before, color, warmth. And there was now--cold, dark, gray.

Had it always been gray?

Sitting with Taylor in church felt gray. Her favorite literature class was gray. Michael's smile at her from across the room was gray.

Gray.

Gray.

Gray.

So she stopped.

The first things to go were Rosario's classes. The coursework stopped flowing. She fell behind in reading here and there, then she missed a class because getting out of bed just felt like too much. In the end it became sleeping in until noon, completely missing an exam that once would have dominated her thoughts for days.

Penelope stopped offering to go get breakfast with her after a week of being shot down. Rosario hadn't responded to Michael or Taylor's texts in days. She'd called Taylor to tell her not to come get her for church a few times now, and she skipped her webcam dates with Peter and Wade.

And then there was today, when Rosario found herself staring at her phone, watching the minutes tick by. Chapel was about to end, and she was cocooned in blankets on her bed. The room wasn't cold, but being wrapped up felt right. She kept off, the only illumination coming from her phone and the laptop in front of her. A notification popped up on her screen.

Penelope: You missed a great chapel. It was so good I even put my homework down long enough to pay attention.

Rosario tried to think of a response. Even the thought of writing back brought a prickle of sweat to the edges of her brow. She set the phone down and refocused on her computer. She was twelve Youtube videos into the archive of a pair of brothers communicating back and forth only through video for a year. The auto play feature of the website brought her through video after video.

At a certain point, she dozed off only to wake up and find them still playing. She could tell she'd missed a few videos since the haircuts of both of the brothers had changed, but she couldn't find it in herself to go back and try and figure out where things stopped, so she just kept going, eyes half open, taking in someone else's life.

The overhead light snapped to life, and Rosario winced. Penelope stood in the doorway.

"Have you been there all day?" she asked.

Rosario nodded before going back to watch the video. She was debating whether or not to pause it when Penelope stepped closer, looming over her. "I am about one second from snapping that thing shut."

Rosario turned up the volume. Penelope huffed and shut the laptop with a snap.

"Hey, what the hell?" Rosario asked, her voice rough with disuse.

"Yeah, what the hell? What's going on with you?"

"Nothing." Rosario pulled her blankets in close as she sat up.

"Okay, then how were classes today?"

"Fine." Rosario looked up at Penelope, but she wasn't giving up any ground. She fixed Rosario with a stare that almost sparked anger within her, but the emotion never broke the surface of the grey all around her.

"What did you eat today?" she continued.

"I had some peanut butter on a banana."

"You had that for breakfast today when I was leaving."

"So?"

"So it's seven at night! The dining hall is closing soon. If you don't hurry up, you won't be able to eat at all."

"I'm not really hungry," Rosario muttered as she lay back down. She opened up her laptop and tapped on the space bar to queue up the video again and Penelope huffed before walking over to her side of the room.

"Can you at least put some headphones on? I need to study."

Rosario could hear the annoyance clear in her voice.

"Sure." Rosario offered a weak smile that she hoped might be read as apologetic. Penelope sighed and handed Rosario the headphones off her desk. She plugged them in and watched as the younger brother began to sing a song about quarks.

Eventually, Rosario got hungry.

A few days passed for her to debate the merits of going to the dining hall, but in the end she opted to run into town for some drive through burgers. They were cheap and the human interaction required was minimal, plus she could go whenever the mood strikes. A few days later Rosario washed down the last of her non-perishable foods with tap water and conceded that perhaps it was time to try something new.

She decided to head out to the twenty-four-hour grocery store in town. It was farther away, but she couldn't imagine facing a busy store during the day. Even the night seemed to be too full for her. The parking lot was near empty, but there were people milling around the front registers and a body in every aisle. She quickly picked her way through the store, her eyes downcast. She grabbed boxes of granola bars, microwave mac and cheese, apples and bananas, juice boxes, lunchables to fill their mini fridge, and a giant tub of trail mix.

Rosario hurried away from the register, weighed down by her purchases, only to run smack into another body on her way out the door. The jar of trail mix fell out of her bag and exploded on the floor in a clatter of shattering plastic pieces.

"Oh! I'm so sorr—Ro?" Taylor placed a gentle hand on Rosario's shoulder, causing Ro to wince. "What are you doing here?"

Rosario stared at Taylor, taking in her wide surprised eyes and half-formed grin.

Then, Rosario burst into tears.

"Ro!" Taylor reached out and wrapped her friend into a hug. "It's okay, we can get more of whatever this stuff is. I'm sorry."

Rosario sobbed harder, falling into her friend's embrace. She let her bags drop to the floor so she could cling to her friend. Taylor held her close and rubbed her back, making soothing noises into her ear.

After a few moments, Rosario pulled away. Taylor examined her face before picking up the discarded bags. "Come on, let's get you out of here."

"But..." Rosario gestured to the mess around her.

"It's okay, ma'am," A helpful man stepped into view, wearing a store apron, with a broom in hand. "I've got it."

"Oh...thanks..." Rosario blinked at him. She waited to feel mortified, but the gray dulled any embarrassment to only a passing thought.

She and Taylor made their way out to Ro's car in silence, only the rustling of the plastic bags in the quiet of the late night. When they get to the car, Rosario fidgeted with her keys.

"What are you doing out so late?" she asked Taylor.

"I could ask you the same thing," Taylor replied. "You look a little rough." There was no malice in her voice, but Rosario bristled at the words all the same.

"Yeah, well, thanks for that." She unlocked her car and reached out to snatchgrab the bags from Taylor. Taylor only handed over half of them, hoisting the rest into the trunk herself. Rosario sighed, closing the trunk with a loud clang.

"Seriously, what's going on?" Taylor stepped into her space and Rosario froze, clenching her hands tightly at her side.

"I..." She searched her friend's face, looking for any sign of judgement but finding only kindness, before finishing. "I don't really know."

Taylor's face softened before she tentatively reached out to urge Rosario in another hug. She melted into the embrace, her hands loosening at her sides. The fight slipped out of her, a pulse of affection breaking through the gray haze, and she let herself be held.

Taylor pulled back, clasping her still by the shoulders.

"Sleepover?" she asked.

Rosario felt her lips twist up without a second thought. "Yeah," she responded. "Sounds good."

With one last hug they parted ways and Rosario got back in her car to follow Taylor across town. They parked on the street and grabbed the bag containing the few perishables Rosario had bought before trudging up the three flights of stairs to Taylors apartment. (Rosario was happy that she only managed to trip once.)

"Home sweet home," Taylor sang as she swung the door open. Her apartment was tidy and decorated in shades of blue and white. It was bright in a way that made Rosario feel like the sun was still up outside. They shoved Rosario's food into the refrigerator and then Taylor rummaged through her drawers, searching for something Rosario could wear. She finds an oversized t-shirt and stretchy yoga pants. They're snug on Rosario, but she was happy to be out of her clothes. If Rosario was being honest she couldn't remember the last time she did laundry.

"Do you want to talk about it?" Taylor asked.

Rosario shook her head, not saying a word. The tension in her muscles started to build, ready to bolt at the threat of confrontation.

"All right," Taylor said mildly. "How about if I talk then?"

Rosario gives her a confused look before nodding.

Taylor launched into a story of what everyone's been up to in the past few weeks. Michael was a guest on a local podcast and everyone had been ribbing him about being too famous for them for days. The joke was starting to wear thin, but it was new to Ro so she almost mustered up a laugh. Then Taylor began to talk about the Korean dramas she'd started watching after Rosario had introduced her to the genre. Rosario laid on the bed and listened, her body slowly relaxing to the lilt of Taylor's speech. Between one word and the next she fell asleep, something almost happy growing in her chest.

—

The next day Rosario swore she would make it to class. She showered quickly, pulling her still damp hair into a high ponytail, before pulling on the least smelly clothes she can find. She had the energy to either go outside or clean, and the anxiety over her grades had crested high enough to get her to forego laundry one more day.

Rosario stepped out into the sun for the first time in days and walked down the lined dirt path toward her first class of the day. She passed by the chapel right as it let out, a wave of talking bodies ran toward her as people made their way to class, and froze. No one around her did anything —people were just talking, laughing, walking in groups up the path toward her—but suddenly her heart was beating so hard she felt it in her teeth.

Rosario spun on her heel and took off running down the path, her breath coming in shallow gasps. The voices followed her, undeterred by her panic, and she veered off the path, stumbling through some shrubs, before sliding down the wall of the nearest building and crouching down behind a tall bush. Rosario thumped her head against the stucco wall and gripped the straps of her bag tight, panic still bubbling up within her. Her emotions were boiling, threatening to spill over into something she couldn't explain, and she couldn't draw in enough air.

She sat like that for long enough that her legs began to cramp before her breath went back to normal. She released the hold on her bag, angry red marks slashed across her palms from the pressure, and felt the dull throb at the back of her head from where she had been pounding it against the wall.

The pain grounded her enough that she could run the short distance to her car and throw it into drive. She sped down the mountain, hands still shaking, until she stopped in front of a familiar townhouse. At the door she fumbled with the key in her hand, letting herself in. No one was home yet—Israel at school, her mother at work—but simply being at home helped calm her.

Kicking off her shoes as she went, she walked into what used to be her room and flopped down on the couch. For a while she laid there, tears slipping down her face, until the door opened.

"Rosario? Are you here?" her mother's voice called. "I saw your car out fr—" Her voice cut off as she rounded the corner and found Rosario on the couch.

She wasn't sure what her mother saw, but the reaction was instant. Her eyes went wide and fearful as she tread into the room.

Rosario would laugh if she could—her mother was treating her like a wounded animal, making her motions clear so she wouldn't spook her. And maybe that's what she was—definitely wounded, probably an animal.

"Mija?" her mother asked. She crouched down in front of her and gently cupped her cheek, thumb rubbing away the tears that slid down her face.

"Mom," Rosario's voice was weak and wavering, but she continued, "I need help."

"What can I do, mija?" Her mother's voice cracked. "I haven't seen you like this since—"

Early this Spring

Rosario sprinted up Richard's driveway, face aching from her huge grin. She knocked on the door rapidly.

Richard opened it, brow furrowed in annoyance, until he saw her face. Richard leaned down to kiss her gently. "Hey you." He pulled back and gestured for her to come inside. "What brings you here? Why didn't you call?"

"Sorry." Rosario was still smiling, unable to keep her joy inside. It must be catching, because Richard's smile grew at the sight.

"What's gotten into you?" he asked.

"I...I got accepted to Mount St. Mary's." Rosario squeaked, jumping up and down in excitement. Richard's face fell and Rosie's stomach dropped.

"I thought we talked about this, Rosie," he whispered, anger seeping into his voice. The happiness Rosario felt still buoyed her forward. He'd be happy once he understood what this meant to her.

"I know, we did, but I applied anyway just to see and—"

"So you lied to me." His voice cut out across the yard. "We had a plan and you decided you didn't want it and you lied—"

"No, no, I didn't—" She sighed in frustration. "The point is I didn't think I'd get in but I did! They even offered me a scholarship! I mean, it's not much, but I didn't even think they'd want me at all."

"Of course not. We both know you don't have what it takes to make it there, Rosie. You're setting yourself up for failure."

"Seriously?" Rosario threw her hands into the air and fought to keep from stamping a foot on the ground. "I thought you'd be happy for me!"

"I know what this means to you, I do." Richard reached out and grabbed her by the hand, lacing their fingers together gently, the touch a sharp contrast to his harsh words. "But I know what you're capable of. I know you struggle just to be average, and I don't want you to waste all this money somewhere where you won't succeed." His voice grew gentle, almost kind. "We have a plan, Rosie; a good plan. Isn't that enough for you?"

"It's just—I've always wanted to go there," she pleaded. "And they accepted me. They must see potential, at least—"

"But I *know you.*" He squeezed her hand tight, too tight. She flinched and tried to draw her hand away but his grip is a vice. "You'll just hurt yourself in the end."

"What if I don't? What if I make it?" Rosario's voice grew louder by the moment. "Will you finally be proud of me then?"

"I'll always be proud of you. But we planned for a future together. Doesn't that mean anything to you? Don't you want to stay together?"

"Of course I do," she replied without hesitation. "But we can still be together, even if I'm far away for a little while. You could save up and move, or we could be long distance. It won't be forever, but—"

"Why are you trying to make things harder for us?!" Richard threw her hand aside and slammed his hand against the wall. "Not only are you sabotaging yourself, you're sabotaging our future. We could be happy together Rosie."

"Why won't you even consider this?" Rosario ran a hand through her hair, tugging . "This is a good thing!"

"YOU'RE NOT BETTER THAN ME!" Richard's voice boomed, the sudden change rocked Rosario to her core.

"I never said I was better than you." Rosario raises her hands in a gesture of surrender. "Why would you even say that?"

"Because you're acting like you're too good for me, for *us*, for this town. You're going to leave and forget all about me and the future we planned together."

"Oh, no, Richard..." In an instant, Rosario was standing by him, reaching up to cradle the side of his neck in her hand, running a soothing hand along the corded muscle there. "I want this life for us together. We can be together, no matter where the future takes us." She ran her thumb over his lips. "I love you, always."

He breaks away from her touch and steps back, eyes dark.

"No, you don't."

"Yes, I do!" Rosario steps forward again, refusing to let him run away. "What do I have to do to prove to you that I love you, that I want to stay with you?"

Richard's eyes were downcast, but as they rose to meet hers, they glinted dangerously.

"You know what you can do." The words carried in the quiet space of the house.

All at once, Rosario realized the house was empty save for the two of them.

Her gut churns.

"No, I don't," she answered, feigning ignorance. In truth, Richard had been bringing it up more and more often, but Rosario felt queasy just at the thought. She wanted it to feel right, and something stopped her every time.

"Then let me show you," Richard murmured as he brought a hand up to cup the back of her neck, tilting her head up to give her lips to him for a deep kiss.

Rosario melted into the moment, kissing back, wanting to pour all the love she feels for him into this one touch, hoping this would be enough. She's so engrossed in the kiss that she almost misses the moment his hand drifts down her back to thumb at the clasp of her bra through the fabric of her shirt.

"What are you doi—" she protested before he kissed her again, this time with force. He fumbled with the hooks before there was a snap, and then her bra fell loose on her arms. She pushed back from him and crossed her arms in front of her chest. "What do you think you're doing?"

"Shhh." Richard ran his hands up and down her tense arms in a soothing slide. "It's okay. You trust me, don't you?"

Rosario froze, unsure of how to respond.

"Don't you?" he asked, hands clamping down on the soft skin of her upper arms.

"I do," she answered, unease flooding through her body, making her limbs shake. "But I don't want this. I've told you before, I'm not ready. I just—"

"You're ready for this. I know you are," Richard murmured as he dipped his head down to kiss along the side of her ear. "We're ready for this..." he trailed off as he lined kisses down her jaw, to her neck, to the junction where her neck and collarbone meet. He knew just how to kiss her to make her go pliant in his hands, so she softened her grip on herself until she felt his hand edge under the hem of her shirt. The touch caused her to tense again, but before she could pull away Richard was crowding into her space, moving her back until she's up against the wall of the hallway.

"Hey, c'mon, I don't want to do this right now." She wiggled a bit, trying to buy some space between the two of them, but Richard slid a hand up just over the middle of her chest and pressed down firmly to keep her in place. She whimpered a bit at the pressure, but he must have mistaken it for a noise of pleasure because he slid a hand up under her until comes up her chest, *too far—*

"You do want this," he whispered in her ear, his voice light and playful. "Your body wouldn't react this way if you didn't."

"I can promise you, I don't want this." Her gut churned and she slid her arms down to shove his hand away. His fingers slid out from under her shirt and she sighed with relief -- but it was short lived. His hands grasped her wrists and raised them high above her head, pinning them to the wall. He grinned wolfishly at her before lowering his mouth again to bite the skin where the collar of her shirt had slipped down her shoulder. She tugged at his hold, and a spark of fear lit up in her chest.

"Don't worry, Rosie, I'll make this good for you," he murmured into her skin before biting down on her shoulder. She screamed at the pressure and he chuckled before pulling back to kiss at the mark. "Mine."

"I'm yours! Always," she assured him, trembling. "You don't need to—"

"Oh, I know." He pulled away to look her in the eye. "But I want to show you how much I love you."

Richard's hand slid back under her shirt, grabbing harshly at her chest, and she winced. He made an amused noise before fingering at the waistband of her yoga pants. The muscles in her stomach jumped at the touch and Rosario struggled with renewed determination.

"If you loved me, you wouldn't do this to me." She sobbed as she fought, struggling to pull her wrists free.

"You don't have to pretend with me, Rosie" He began to slide her pants down past her hips. Nausea washed over her. She didn't want this. She wasn't ready. She needed to get out. "I know what you want. You don't have to feel ashamed. I don't care what your parents think, what your God says, I know what you want and what is right for us. We're in love, we can show each other how much we—"

With as much force as she could muster, Rosario stomped down on the top of Richard's foot. He roared in pain, his fingers loosening just enough to allow her to get free. She shoved him as hard as she could and he stumbled a few feet back. Rosario darted toward the door, but she only sprinted a few feet, and his hands yank her in.

"You bitch," he growled as he dragged her. "You're going to regret doing that."

Rosario couldn't get free.

Richard shoved her to the ground and she landed with a thump on the entryway tile. He leered over her, teeth sharp and white.

With one last burst of strength, Rosario lifted her leg, kicking him straight in the groin.

He doubled over, groaning, and she scrambled for the door. As the handle turned, Richard cursed behind her, struggling to stand.

For a moment Rosario fumbled with the door, knob shaking in her unsteady grasp, before suddenly it clicked and swung wide open. Rosario ran down the street, keys shaking in her hand, early afternoon sun blinding her. The car unlocked from a few feet away and she slid into the front seat, making sure to lock it as soon as possible.

Rosario turned the key and the car clicked a few times but nothing else happened. Panic bloomed in her chest, but another deft turn of the key and the engine turned over. Rosario let out a breath and peeled out of the quiet neighborhood, speeding all the way home. She parked the car and jumped out, running for the door and not stopping until it's locked and bolted behind her. She slid to the floor just as her mother rounded the corner carrying a basket of laundry on her hip.

"Mija!" her mother yelled, dropping the basket and rushing to her side. She reached out to grab her and Rosario flinched, pushing her mother away.

Stunned, her mother lets it happen, face ashen as she took in the sight before her. Rosario can't imagine what she saw—tear stained face, maybe a shadow of the bite on her shoulder, clothes pulled apart, bruises forming on her wrists.

"What happened?" her mother whispered, her voice shaking.

Rosario simply stared at her mother, at her concerned face, and let the tears flow freely.

Rosario stayed at her mother's house for a few days before she found herself scheduling an appointment with the campus therapy center. Her mother only mentioned it once since she'd come home, but the thought stayed pinned in her brain.

With every passing gray moment, she thought of it more and more. The videos of the two brothers were becoming more and more current—soon she would reach the end, and then what would she do? Booking the appointment takes only a moment—her student ID number, phone number, pick a time, done. Then she was back to watching the videos. Her mother put them up on the big TV in the living room and Rosario sat there, eyes glazed over, as she watched one discuss a crisis in Syria.

Her mother sat beside her, bringing with her steaming bowl of arroz con pollo. Rosario took it gratefully as her mother settled in on the opposite end of the couch. Normally they'd be pressed together, sharing the same blanket, but since she's been home, her mother has been careful to give her space. Rosario doesn't know how to tell her that things are different this time, that before she was scared of touch and now she's thirsty for it, so she simply eats her food in slow, measured bites.

The videos roll one after another. At some point, her mother stood and made her way back to the kitchen to clean up. Rosario paused the video to take a nap, exhausted already at the prospect of talking to someone tomorrow, and when she wakes, it's to her childhood blanket tucked tightly around her.

—

When Rosario arrived back at the dorm Penelope had both headphones in, loud music seeping out into the air. Rosario tapped her lightly on the shoulder and Penelope jolted, whipping around and ripping the headphones from her hears.

"Hey…" Rosario said as she fiddled with the sleeve of her sweater. "I'm back?" A beat of silence passed, but then Penelope was on her feet, chair toppled over, and she hugged Rosario tightly.

"You showered," she said, her voice shaky with tears.

"Yeah...it was time." Rosario shrugged. They both laughed in relief, glad in this moment to be back together. When it was time for Rosario's appointment Penelope walked down with her to the counseling center and sat in the waiting room to keep her company without probing for why she'd come in the first place. Rosario was immensely grateful that she didn't have to talk about it again, that Penelope was the kind of friend that could just be there for someone.

But she could do without the talk about the Spring Formal.

"PLeeeeeSEEE!" Penelope whined.

"I'm not really a dance person," Rosario replied.

"Oh, me neither," Penelope assured her, "But it's still fun. You get to dress up and go to dinner and take fun pictures. I'm part of the planning committee so I can promise it won't be lame."

"I'm not sure if you can keep that promise," Rosario said.

Penelope rolled her eyes and changed the subject, talking about the latest drama happening in their dorm.

After a few more minutes of listening to Penelope ramble on excitedly, a kind lady called Rosario's name from the hallway. Rosario followed her back to a room around the corner before she came face to face with a jovial looking man in his sixties. He had a big, white beard and wire-rimmed glasses, and for a moment, Rosario has to bite her lips to keep from calling him Santa.

"Hello, my name is Ford." He moved aside and gestured for her to enter the room. "Please come in."

Rosario took a few timid steps in and looked at the room before her. A big wooden desk with a large leather chair dominated one end of the room. Papers and books piled high on top of the desk, and a bookshelf completes the picture. A big plush couch spanned an otherwise empty wall and in the corner there was a small side table with a hot water kettle, mugs, and a variety of pouches.

"Help yourself to some tea; I just need to tidy up my desk a bit."

While Ford shuffled papers at his desk, Rosario examined the offered tea. Over ten different kinds of tea all crowded the same mason jar. She grabbed one at random, pulling out a spicy cinnamon-scented satchel. She poured pre-boiled water over the bag in her mug and brought it to the couch with her. She wedged herself into the corner, putting a big pillow in her lap, and watched as Ford pulled out a clipboard.

"Alright, Rosario, what brings you in today?" he asked, voice sincere, eyes warm.

Rosario opened her mouth and everything fell out.

Michael. Taylor. Richard. Moving. School. The gray. Her dad, and the pain of him being gone. She left it all on the floor between them, the words jagged and cutting through her gray to tear her up inside.

CHAPTER NINE

Praying--Kesha

Ford recommended that Rosario go outside every day, for 30 minutes a day. There were no other requirements other than that—for now, Ford promised—and Rosario sat in her room struggling with the thought. It was almost ten at night, and she reasoned that most people would be in their dorms getting ready for sleep now, like Penelope, who rummaged through her drawers beside Ro.

"I swear I just washed my TARDIS sleep pants," she muttered to herself as she closed the drawer, an obviously second tier pair of plain black pants in her hands.

"You wore them on laundry day," Rosario offered from where she'd been sitting, perched stiffly on the edge of her bed.

"Oh." Penelope frowned. "Well, nevermind. Thanks, Ro. Why aren't you getting ready for bed?"

Rosario considered lying, before she sighed and said, "My thera—Ford. He said I should go outside once a day, for thirty minutes." She fidgeted with the edge of her comforter before standing. "I'm going to go now."

"Mind some company?" Penelope asked. She set her clothes down on her desk.

"What?" Rosario blinked in confusion. "No, you don't -- I mean...I can go alone. Don't feel like you have to—"

"I don't have to do anything, you know," Penelope pulled on a pair of Vans. "Come on, the campus cafe closes in thirty minutes. If we hurry, we can grab some hot chocolate."

Rosario rolled her eyes fondly. Penelope finished getting ready, and together they made their way down to the campus cafe. It was a Tuesday, and the late hour wasn't near any major testing times, so the cafe was quiet and only housed a handful of people tapping away on laptops. Still, Rosario tensed in the doorway. Penelope stopped behind her, not pushing her in but enough of a presence that Rosario shook herself and continued to the counter.

"Two hot chocolates, please," she muttered, self-conscious of the waver in her voice.

The barista seemed too bored to notice her reaction and waved them on as they began putting together their drinks.

"Oh my lord, by the way, the last time I was here I was on the most *terrible* date. She was cute, but I swear she could not stop interrupting me."

"You do talk a lot when you're nervous," Rosario offered.

"Which is a great reason why her interrupting was a cosmic sign that we were just not meant to be." Penelope handed Rosario her drink and tapped her scuffed checkerboard shoe against the tile floor, waiting for her own drink. "But then she spilled her coffee all over my Betsy Johnson dress--you know, the one with the glitter?--and she didn't even offer me a napkin!"

"No," Rosario gasped, choking on the warm liquid.

"Can you believe that?" Penelope laughed and grabbed her beverage from the barista. "I mean, I knew chivalry was dead, but that is just sad."

"She probably thought you were a strong, independent woman who could take care of herself," Rosario snarked with a smirk.

"Ha. Ha. So. Funny." Penelope rolled her eyes and took a sip of her drink.

They walked around the campus in a companionable silence until the trees grew dense and Rosario realized she was leading them somewhere. She stopped short and Penelope froze next to her.

"Ro? Everything okay?" Penelope asked.

Rosario debated going back for a moment, simply turning around and keeping this secret spot a secret, but something in her ached to go back there, to chase the memory of those warm feelings back again. So she shook her head and led her friend through the brush and into the clearing.

The night held more of a chill than it had before, but almost everything else was the same. A few notable changes had taken place--there were piles of balanced stones near one end of the clearing, and someone had arranged sticks into the outline of two bodies holding hands.

Rosario set her half full cup down on a stone and laid down in the middle of the clearing.

After a few moments, Penelope sat down next to her and tipped her gaze to the sky. They stayed like that for a while, Rosario breathing in deep, before she stood and dusted herself off.

For a moment, the memory of Michael's hand grasping hers gently cut through the lingering gray inside of her, but she sighed and it was gone.

Rosario and Penelope's walks down to the clearing became a nightly tradition. Penelope took to brewing a thermos of tea on her own that they share. As classes picked up, they brought down a small camping lantern Rosario bought from Walmart, along with a blanket and their readings for class, and they stayed out under the stars to do some work. The silence did wonders for Rosario's peace of mind. Between her time outside and her sessions with Ford, she began to live a peaceful co-existence with the gray inside of her.

"Feeling gray is no way to live," Ford tells her one day in late March. "I want to try something new."

"Oh no," Rosario groans into the rim of her mug. "What? More outside time?"

"No, I want you to go see a psychiatrist."

"I'm not crazy." Rosario shot up in her seat and glared at Ford, betrayal stinging her lungs.

"I didn't say you were." He lifted his hands in a placating gesture. "But there might be something out there to help you with that gray feeling."

Rosario stayed silent, mulling the thought over in her head.

"So, how are classes going?" Ford asked, letting the subject drop.

"Can we go back to talking about the psychiatrist?" Rosario whined.

"That bad, huh?"

"I missed so much, Ford. I don't know how I'll ever catch up. It all feels so...hopeless."

"I think I know someone who can help with that too."

"Oh, let me guess -- is it a psychiatrist?" Rosario snarked.

Ford gave a very Santa-esque belly laugh.

"No, we have a coordinator on campus that could help you. She could reach out to your teachers and come up with an alternate solution to your issues."

"I'll think about it." Rosario gave in after a few minutes of silence.

Ford nodded and took out a pad of paper, writing for a few minutes before handing the slip over to her. It has two names—'Jamara Philips, disability coordinator. Billie Gordon—psychiatrist'—and Rosario slipped the paper into her pocket before standing.

Ford saw her out with a smile and Rosario felt the weight of the numbers in her pocket like an anchor.

The dreams start the next night.

Algebra II is going on all around her, but all she can think about is the phone in front of her. A new message pops on the screen.

Richard: Can I see you tonight?

Rosario smiled and bites her lip before writing back.

Rosario: Can't, sorry. I'm busy. Maybe next time? <3

The text bubble pops up, then goes away, then comes back before—

Richard: Hopefully next time is soon.

Rosario tried to give the class the rest of her attention, but the bell rings and then she was out on the field to run a mile in gym class. She was sweating and heaving for breath at the end of the class, and as she made her way out of the locker room and toward the front of the school, she's buoyed by the thought that Richard might want to spend time with her.

Once she was out of the front gate, getting ready to put her headphones in, Rosario saw Richard standing in the crowd, leaning against his big gray truck. He caught her eye over the throng of people and waved.

With a laugh, she ran over to his side, cutting through the crowds without a care.

"What are you doing here?" Rosario asked breathlessly. Richard grinned down at her and opened his arms, waiting. Rosario laughed again and pulled him into a hug that he returned tightly.

"You said you were busy tonight, so I thought at least I could see if I could take you home. We could spend some time together on the drive?"

"Richard, it's like two stop lights away," Rosario said, secretly pleased that he'd come all this way to get her. He had just started at the local community college across town -- the fact that he came all this way just to see her lit her up inside. They had only been dating for a week, so the feeling was new and unique.

"That is two whole stop lights I get to spend with the prettiest girl around." He pulled away after a kiss to the top of her head and walked around to the other side of the truck, opening the door for her. She blushed and slid into the vehicle, setting her bag on the ground.

As Rosario buckled in, Richard climbed into the driver's side, starting the truck with a roar. Instantly music blared to life, a solid bass rumble filling the cab. He lowered the volume with a sheepish smile before pulling out of the parking lot.

Rosario chatted animatedly about her day and craft she wanted to do with Israel to give to their mother for her birthday. He nodded along, prodding for more information about the birthday festivities, until they came to a stop in front of her house.

"Here, let me get the door for you," Richard said before hopping out of his seat. He helped her down and scooped up her bag. Rosario pulled her house key from her pocket and paused in the doorway.

"You can come in, if you want." She grinned shyly up at him. "I can make pizza bagels."

"Tempting. Would these pizza bagels happen to be mini sized?"

"No, I'm not heathen," Rosario countered playfully. "I make my own homemade, full-size pizza bagels, thank you very much."

"Oh, this I've got to see." Richard followed her inside. It smelled of warm spices and laundry detergent and home, and Richard seemed to slot into place inside it.

They worked well together in the kitchen, moving seamlessly as they gathered ingredients and putting together an easy snack. They sat at the breakfast bar side by side, sharing a plate between them, their feet bumping together as they dangled from the bar stool.

After they finished eating, Richard made his way to the door.

"You don't have to go if you don't want to," Rosario offered. His hand was on the knob, and he turned slightly to face her.

"I know your mom isn't home, and I know I really like you." He began fondly. "And I don't want to do anything to mess this up. So I think, for now, it's best if I head home."

Rosario wrapped him in her arms for a tight hug. Richard dropped a soft kiss to her lips. The touch is chaste and sweet, but too soon, they're separated.

Richard headed out of the door. She stood in the doorway and watched him drive away, a bright smile tugging at her still kiss warmed lips.

Rosario woke with a start, heart thudding in her chest.

The memory makes her warm, cutting through the gray haze.

Rosario took a deep breath, held it for two counts, and exhaled through her mouth--a trick Ford taught her in therapy. And then, she dove into the dream. Because it was a dream. Richard's truck was small and white and beat up, he never went to college, still too angry about missing out on wrestling scholarships years later, and that first time in her home he had been awkward, unwilling to help and demanding to be served. She could see it all now with hindsight, but her dreams sought to comfort her and she desperately needed it. Anything to cut through the gray.

After over a week of constant dreams of Richard, Rosario made the call to talk to a psychiatrist.

Nothing cut through the gray like those dreams, dreams that dragged her from blissful, sweet memories to dark, truthful pain. She couldn't take another night of remembering what she gave up, what turned on her and made her walk away. Each night she had to face the girl who dreamed of a life with someone and reconcile that with the reality where his hands turned harsh and crushing and drove her away.

Rosario ended up telling Ford about everything, all the dreams and how they make her feel. He listened in silence, not judging a word she said, and only asked her one thing.

"When are you going to talk to that psychiatrist?"

So she called.

The appointment was a few days later in a sleek office downtown.

The psychiatrist, Billie, was a woman in her forties with a short platinum asymmetrical bob. Unyielding blue eyes appraised Rosario, and for a moment, Rosario bristled under the attention.

Rosario left with a prescription for an antidepressant and an appointment for six weeks out. She sighed heavily once the door closed behind her. Rosario hoped that she could simply power through this, that she could fight her way past the bad memories and up through all the gray, but the paper in her grasp felt like a relief. A hand reaching down into the gray, offering to help pull her up.

She would take it gladly.

The next thing on her list was seeing the disability coordinator. She fought it for as long as she could, but one night out in the field with Penelope brought her situation into focus.

"Can you believe we're already thinking about finals? It's barely April!" Penelope flopped onto her back. "My statistics teacher put out a tool you can use to calculate what grade you'll need on the final to pass any class. All you do is put the numbers in and hit a button and it does all the work for you."

"Shouldn't you be the one doing the work, statistics girl?" Rosario raised an eyebrow at her, but Penelope only rolled her eyes.

"If I'm not getting graded on it, I'll let someone else do the work."

When they returned back to the dorm, Rosario pulled up the grade calculator on her computer and punched in the information she had. The results were grim. No matter which way she cut it her grades can't be salvaged. She brought the tool down to her next meeting with Ford and he looked over the numbers with her.

"I've been working so hard, as hard as I can." Rosario ran a nervous hand through her hair and tugged at the ends. "I've been going to classes, I haven't missed one in weeks, but I'm still failing."

"You've got a lot to make up for, it's true." Ford adjusted his glasses. "But I think I know where we can get some help."

The next day, she found herself sitting in an administration building, waiting on plush leather seating.

"Rosario?" a voice called from down the hall.

Rosario turned to follow the noise only to come face to face with Michael's ex girlfriend, Jamara. She had forgotten about that time all those weeks ago when Taylor had pointed her out, but she seemed just as stunning now as she was then. Her hair was now loose around her face, but her smile was bright and welcoming. Rosario was too thrown by the encounter to begin for a moment.

Once they were seated, Jamara leaned over her desk and smiled. "Whenever you're ready, just tell me what you need."

"I...missed a lot of class," she began. "I know that's probably self-explanatory. I mean why would I be here if I wasn't having a problem with classes, right? Yeah. Anyway. I just—" Rosario stopped herself and took a deep breath in for seven seconds, paused, and then let it out for seven seconds, just like Ford taught her. Then she began again. "Ford recommended I come talk to you. He's my therapist."

"He's a good man. He's helped lots of people on this campus," Jamara offered.

"He's been helping me work through some stuff. I couldn't get to class for a long time. I'm doing better now, but..." she trailed off, having a hard time actually saying the words.

"But you think it's too late?" Jamara finished for her.

Rosario nodded solemnly.

"Let me be the judge of that," Jamara said.

Together, they worked on a plan. Jamara got permission from Rosario to speak with her teachers about her mental health struggles and Jamara formulated a plan to propose to them that would allow her an opportunity to recover the ground she'd lost.

Rosario left the office feeling lighter. Being around Jamara wasn't hard; she was a bright presence that had made her feel welcome. In that moment, Rosario knew what Michael must have liked about her, but jealousy didn't overtake her as it had before. If anything, sadness filled her that Michael had to end a relationship with someone who seemed so kind and wonderful. She remembered Taylor's comment about Michael getting his heart crushed and paused.

Thanks to a combination of Richard isolating her and Rosario trying her best to highlight all the good things about him to others, Richard probably seemed perfect to everyone when they were dating, but that had been a lie. Certainly some part of Richard had been just as fun and loving as people had seen, but inside there was a darkness that had burned them both. She shuddered away from the thought and walked out into the warming spring air, eager to put the past behind her.

That Sunday was her first back in church. Taylor had long since stopped offering to drive her, so this time she joined her mother and Israel on the drive down. Each winding turn through the tree lined drive there amped up her excitement and a cheer went up at her arrival when she stepped out of her mother's car.

"Oh my god, it's Ro!" Scott yelled from the front of the building.

Rosario laughed, waving hello as she grabbed her bag from the back of the car. The whole group gathered around her, each one hugging her in turn.

"I'm so glad to see you." Michael grinned as he wrapped his arms around her tightly. She blushed and clung to him desperately for a moment, the butterflies she felt around him piercing through the gray that still hung a bit around her heart. Panic clutched at her throat as she realized the feeling was similar to how she felt upon waking from dreams of Richard. But, as Ford liked to say, it was time to examine the evidence. Michael was gentle and fond, sincere and kind. These feelings for him were similar, yes, but *he* wasn't, and that made all the difference.

"I'm glad to be here," Rosario said honestly. They stayed like that for a moment before all walking inside.

Michael headed up to the front for worship, picking his guitar up on the way, before he took his place on the stage.

"Michael isn't with the kids today?" Rosario asked, looking around to see all the children still seated with their families.

"He's preaching today! You came back at just the right time." Taylor waggled her eyebrows at Rosario and she rolled her eyes fondly. Church was not the time for flirting...right? Throughout the songs, their eyes kept finding each other. At first they glanced away quickly, Rosario's cheeks heating. But, after about the third time their eyes met, Michael smiled widely, biting back a laugh. Rosario shook her head, unable to stop her own smile from pulling at her cheeks.

The church service itself goes by in a blur, Michael's words flow around her like water, rolling off her in droplets and only half way soaking in. Mostly, Rosario basked in the feeling of being surrounded by people she loves and cares about, and knowing they love and care for her too.

As the service ended and they began to make their way back outside, Taylor came up to Rosario's side and looped an arm through hers.

"Michael sure seemed happy to see you," she began, a sly smile in place.

"Did he?" Rosario feigned innocence. "I didn't really notice."

Out of the corner of her eye, Rosario saw Taylor roll her eyes.

"Well, he's been asking about you a lot." Taylor steered them outside and under an awning in the shade. Outside several people turned to wave at them, all smiling and calling out their joy at seeing Rosario return. "When you stopped replying to his messages, he thought he had done something wrong."

"What?" Rosario stopped short. "Did he really?"

Taylor nodded. "I told him you weren't talking to me either. We were both pretty worried until that night I ran into you. I let him know you had other stuff going on."

Rosario mulled over this as the crowd moved around her. She hadn't stopped to think about her silence impacting other people. To her the gray was all encompassing, but to her friends,it must have seemed like something else entirely. Before her train of thought could turn any more melancholy it was interrupted by Michael sprinting out of the church door and barreling toward them.

"Ro! I was worried you'd taken off already," Michael said, a little breathless.

"Nope, I'm still here." Rosario shrugged. "Don't you have to go help put away the band stuff?."

"In a minute." He fidgeted before looking away. "I don't think we'll all be going to lunch today, but maybe I could drive you back to your dorm?"

"Uh, sure..." Rosario glanced toward Taylor. She nodded enthusiastically and Rosario had to bite back a laugh.

"Why don't I help you pick stuff up then?" Rosario offered.

"That'd be awesome." Michael motioned for her to follow him back inside the church. Rosario parted ways with Taylor after a hug and a whispered promise that they'd call and talk once Rosario made it home.

Michael and Rosario spent the better part of an hour putting away equipment, cleaning classrooms, and talking about everything that had happened since they'd last seen each other.

"We all went on another hike to the falls," Michael supplied as he walked past her to check the locks on the windows. "No one went into the water though. It was way too cold."

Rosario thought she heard something similar to 'we missed you' unspoken, but she only hummed in response. She heard Michael stop moving things around before his footfalls approached, coming to stop a few inches behind her. She turned and found his hand raised in mid-air, almost as if he was reaching out to her. She flinched away instinctively, and the concern in his face took her aback.

"I...I was worried about you," he whispered, but his voice carried loudly in the empty church space. They were the last ones left in the building. Their closeness opened something within her, something vulnerable and secure at the same time.

"I was worried about me too," she murmured, raw with honesty. "I missed you." Michael dropped his hand on her shoulder to squeeze her gently. She warmed to the touch, a small smile lifting the corners of her mouth.

"I think we're done here," Michael said. He gestured for her to follow him to the door. Their conversation went back to being light and teasing. It was easy to fall into a rhythm of happy chatter as they got into his beat up old Honda and drove away from the church. There, their conversation drifted into companionable silence.

Michael handed her his phone.

"Pick out something to listen to, I always have to have a soundtrack when I drive," he said.

The background on his phone was a picture of her, Michael, and Kathryn sitting together outside by the fire pit at Kathryn's parent's house. The yellow light of the fire made the photo look cozier than she remembered it being. They'd all been bundled up against the chilly air, but from the color high in Rosario's cheeks you'd think it had been a balmy night.

Mortification filled Rosario at her face in the picture. She was gazing toward Michael, and embarrassment rooted in her stomach at the look of pure adoration on her face. Rosario winced and prayed that Michael hadn't noticed. She reassured herself he wouldn't use it as his phone background if he knew how she felt, and distracted herself by picking out some songs. A brief perusal through his phone told her that they had remarkably similar music taste--a bunch of alt rock with top forty hits sprinkled throughout. She tapped through a few screens until she landed on a series of playlists he had set up. The titles were mostly obvious—a work out playlist, the party song list they have all shared on their devices, a few lists of songs from different movies—but there was a single list that caught her eye.

The playlist was entitled "same." Rosario tapped the title and scrolled through the list of songs before queueing one up.

"I love this song," Rosario said as the first few chords fill the car. "It's crazy, you have the version that's a cover by Motion City Soundtrack, my favorite band. I didn't think many people knew about it."

"It's a good song," Michael gave her a strange smile.

"All the songs in this playlist are great, actually," Rosario offered as she continued scrolling through the titles. "It's kind of amazing how perfect they are. Can you share this with me?"

"Sure," Michael said, laughing softly to himself.

Rosario looked at him oddly. "What's so funny?" she asked.

"Nothing," he replied, and returned his attention to the road.

After a moment, Rosario shrugged and went back to tapping through Michael's music collection. She kept playing "same.", humming along to each song that passed before they pulled up into a spot outside of her dorm.

As Michael cut the engine, he asked, "Can I walk you inside?"

"Of course," Rosario smiled--she never could stop smiling around Michael.

They made their way up the stairs while Rosario recounted a story about the last time Penelope had been out at the spring formal meetings and someone had tripped while walking up the stairs in a way that made even Rosario seem graceful. Michael laughed and made a show of guiding Rosario up the rest of the stairs, as if she was prone to falling at any moment. "You know it wasn't me that fell, right?"

"I know, but I also have seen your shins bruised up enough times to know that it just as easily could have been you."

Rosario huffed, but savored the warmth of his hand hovering just above the small of her back.

"Come on in," Rosario beckoned once they'd reached her door. She watched as Michael made his way over to her guitar. He strummed a few chords.

"You want to give it a shot?"

"Me?" Rosario squeaked.

"Yeah, you." He chuckled. "I did promise you I'd teach you a while back."

"That's true..." Rosario looked down and tugged at the hem of her shirt. "But I'm not sure about this right now."

"What's wrong?" Michael asked, brow furrowed

"It's just..." Rosario ran a hand through her hair. "I'm a bit nervous."

"Nervous? Why?"

"Because you're so good at this and I'm...totally going to suck." Rosario sat down hard on the end of her bed, leaning her elbows on her knees and putting her head in her hands.

"Hey, it's okay," Michael dropped down next to her. "I definitely understand; believe me. But I want you to know I'd never judge you, alright?"

Rosario peeked up from her hands to gauge his reaction. He was smiling down at her reassuringly, and her heart regained courage. She nodded up at him and his smile grew. "I'll start real simple and then you can tell me if you're ready for more. Is that okay?"

"Alright," Rosario agreed, straightening. "Let's do it."

"Awesome." Michael grabbed the guitar from where he'd left it and sat beside her once again. "So these are the names of the strings..." He named off each one as he plucked them.

Rosario repeated them back and he nodded encouragingly.

"These are called frets," he continued, gesturing to the metal sections on the neck of the guitar. "You press the strings down between the frets and you make a chord." He arranged his fingers before strumming out a sweet, resonating tone. "Then you put a bunch of chords together and strum them in a certain pattern and that's the basics of playing a song."

"Alright." Rosario fussed with her cuticles.

"If you want, I can show you how to play a few chords," Michael volunteered.

"Sure," Rosario said. He handed her the guitar and she picked it up and attempted to hold it the way she had seen him do it. Michael reached out and gently moved her positioning. The light pressure of his fingers sent goosebumps up her arms. She flushed at her body's obvious response and prayed Michael didn't notice.

"Now put your first finger on the third fret of the second string, your second finger on the second fret of the third string, and your third finger on the first fret of the fourth string."

"Uh..." Rosario looked owlishly up at him.

"Move this finger here." Michael used his long, calloused fingers to softly move her to the correct strings. "This is your second string, remember?"

"Right," Rosario nodded. "And this is the second fret, so that means I need to move this to here."

"Exactly."

Rosario was abruptly struck by how close together they were-- faces close enough to almost feel the breath moving between them. Michael's fingers twitched minutely, his calloused grip tightening around her.

Rosario could feel warmth in her cheeks, but at this distance she could see a matching hue rising up on Michael's face. Their eyes held each other for a moment and she searched his gaze, trying to decipher what she saw, hoping to see her own feelings reflected there, but instead she got caught up in the too-blue hue she saw there. His eyes darted down for a moment before fluttering closed.

Then, suddenly, there was nothing but cold air in front of her.

Michael stood by the opposite side of the bed, hands shoved in his pockets, eyes wide. Rosario looked at the empty spot where he once was, then up again at Michael but when she tried to meet his eyes he glanced away.

"I should get going," Michael said, the words rushing from his mouth. "We definitely need to restring your guitar before we keep going. It—yeah. We can't keep going. Not now." He began to edge toward the door. "I'm so glad I got to see you today. But, yeah, I have to go. I'll text you, okay?"

Michael rushed out the door.

Rosario blinked slowly, trying to process what just happened. Her fingers were still carefully holding a C chord, the faint memory of Michael's warm hand on hers lingering there with her.

That night, instead of Richard, she dreams of calloused fingers guiding hers and a bright blue inscrutable gaze.

CHAPTER TEN

Stupid Love -- Lady Gaga

Rosario feels the gray lifting day by day, and with each new hue returning to her she does her best to move forward to get back to where she used to be. Despite her initial misgivings,deciding to take medication had been a huge step forward.

Ford agreed the best way for her to begin to manage relationships again was by texting. The interactions would be less taxing than going out all at once again, but even juggling multiple conversations had been exhausting.

For instance -- the exchange she was having with Wade and Peter at this moment. They were trying to plan what to get Kamala for her upcoming birthday and the flurry of messages overwhelmed Rosario.

Peter: I think we should send flowers to her work.

Wade: Flowers die, Peter.

Peter: Everything dies, Wade.

Rosario: Wow.

Wade: Wow.

Peter: What?

Peter: Too honest?

Wade: I mean,,,, we're talking about a birthday here,,,, Shouldn't we be avoiding mentions of death???

Peter: OR maybe we should be mentioning death. Like, hooray you haven't died yet!

Rosario: W O W

Peter: Okay so no on the flowers then?

Wade: Yeah I think that's a no.

Rosario: Yeah no on your death flowers. Save them for our funerals.

Peter: Alright so which one of you has a better idea?

Rosario: Well I know now that she's in her own place she's really been into cooking right?

Wade: Pork of the month club!

Rosario: Wade, no.

Peter: We're trying to do something nice for her. It is not nice to directly insult her religion.

Wade: Okay, okay, I was just trying to out-terrible Mr. Death Flowers over here

Peter: Flowers are a perfectly normal and nice present!

Wade: you're right. I love when you give me flowers. *heart eyes emoji*

Peter: I have never once given you flowers

Wade: HINT HINT

Rosario: Well I have to go to class. But, before I go, I vote for a waffle maker.

Rosario silenced her phone before sliding it into her backpack and taking off toward chapel. She met up with Penelope along the way and listened to her chat about her committee meeting while they pushed through the groups of students waiting to get inside. They grabbed their slips of paper and made their way to the top of the bleachers in the back corner. It was the perfect spot for doing your homework. No one could sit behind you and judge you for having your laptop out during the service. Penelope pulled out a large tome on organic chemistry and a thick packet of papers before hunkering down and getting to work.

Rosario began annotating a small book of poems in preparation for class discussion. She was working on the sonnets for next week, trying her best to not fall behind in the crucial last few classes before their final exams.

After an hour of listening to the service while jotting down notes in the margins of her books, Rosario made her way to her literature class. As she walked in the professor gave her an appraising look.

"Rosario, can you come speak with me after class?" he called.

"Of course." Heat ran up the back of Rosario's neck as she settled in the back of the room, intent on hiding behind her book for the rest of the hour. She fought to pay attention, but all she could do was think over what the professor might need to talk with her about. He'd already agreed to the terms Jamara had outlined weeks ago, and she'd been doing extra work to make sure she stayed on target to complete the term.

When class ended, Rosario watched as the rest of the students filed out in small groups. Once the room cleared, she stood and walked to the podium.

"You wanted to talk to me?" She asked, tugging at the strap of her backpack.

"Rosario, I ran into Dr. Crawford, he's your philosophy professor, correct? He told me he's making you write an extra paper for your make up work."

"That's right." Rosario worked on the outline just the night before.

"That makes three papers before the end of the term if you include the make up essay I assigned you, plus the final ten page paper we're doing in class."

"Yes," Rosario confirmed.

"That seems like a lot of writing. I'd hate to have you give anything less than your best on your final for this class."

"Oh, well, I understand your worry completely, but I promise I'll give this final everything I possibly can."

"I don't doubt it. But regardless that is a lot to cover in such a short span of time. I was thinking, instead of the make up paper, I assign an alternative."

"Excuse me?" Rosario asked. Panic rushed down her spine. Something about this triggered every anxious memory of Richard's hands on her.

"Well, how about we have a verbal quiz instead?"

"A...verbal quiz?" Rosario parroted.

"Essentially we'd be discussing everything we'd covered this semester. Nothing is off limits, no reference materials would be allowed, but it'd be an accurate way to gauge your understanding of the course materials without making you take up extra hours you could spend writing for your final. I'd still require the passage analysis paper that is your final exam, but this verbal quiz would replace the extra paper I'd assigned you."

"I—uh, that sounds great!" Rosario said, still processing the change. Not everyone was like Richard, it seemed. "I would really appreciate that."

"Excellent. Does Saturday work for you?"

"Did you mean this Saturday?" She mentally counted the days between today and the weekend and there simply were not enough.

"I will get quite busy grading for these final exams, so I was hoping we could get this out of the way as soon as possible."

"Right," Rosario agreed hastily, not wanting to waste the opportunity she had been given. "Of course. Saturday works for me."

"Alright. I'll see you at my office at ten AM, if that works for your schedule."

"It does, definitely." Rosario said gratefully, waving Dr. Randal before parting ways. She had a lot of studying to do between today and the final, but the thought of the free time she'd have once the work was out of the way was motivation enough.

For the next several nights, Rosario and Penelope spent their time in the clearing on campus quizzing each other. Rosario laid on her back, face tilted to the sky, and recited facts and information as best she could while taking comfort from the surroundings that had become like a second home to her. Rosario recited back dates and information, and eventually she felt as prepared as she was going to get for the coming exam.

"Alright, who was your favorite character this semester?" Dr. Randal begins, peering at her from over a cup of steaming coffee in his hands.

"Uh...what?" Rosario cleared her throat. "I'm sorry. I'm confused."

"Your favorite character. I want to know who you like and why."

"Uh..." Rosario combed through her consciousness for opinions, but all she had crammed in where dates and facts. In desperation she closed her eyes, took a deep breath, and threw it all away. "I like Lady Macbeth. She's crazy."

Her professor's eyes lit up, and just like that, a conversation began. They spoke about themes and historical relevance, but it flowed naturally from talking about favorite scenes and recurring symbols. By the end of two hours, Rosario felt confident in her understanding of the class and engaged in a way she hadn't been before.

"So are you more prepared to take on your final paper now?" Dr. Randal asked.

"I think so, actually." Rosario laughs. "I think that might have been your plan all along."

"Perhaps." Dr. Randal stood and gestured for her to follow him out. "But I will say that you've probably produced more engaging information today that most of your fellow classmates have all semester. Have a great rest of your day, Rosario."

"You too!" She called happily as she jogged back across campus to her dorm, buoyed by the success of the day.

Once she returned back to her room, she saw a text from Kamala. She opened it up to find a picture of a shiny immersion blender on top of her countertop with the caption "Best birthday present ever!"

Rosario typed out a response, happy the present they got for her turned out to be something she wanted.

Just as she sent out her text, another came in from Michael.

Michael: Hey Ro! How did the exam go?

Rosario: I think it went pretty good! I won't really know until grades come in, but it was a good conversation.

Michael: Yeah, he is a good guy. I'm sure you did great.

Rosario smiled down at her phone and shook her head.

Rosario: Of course you're on a first name basis with my English professor.

Michael: Hey, he was my professor first. Plus, he plays killer bass. We used to play together in a small jazz band on campus.

Rosario: Alright, this is officially too weird. I can't even picture you in a jazz band.

A few moments went by before a picture message loaded in. A group of people dressed to the nines were arranged around one another in what must be the performance area for the music department. Sure enough Michael was holding his guitar next to where Rosario's professor was standing with a bass in his hands.Michael's hair was longer and had blue streaks through it and Rosario could just imagine him hamming it up on stage.

Michael: Is it still weird now that you don't have to try and picture it?

Rosario: It might be even weirder.

Michael: Let me make it up to you. How about you come over and hang out, now that you've got a bit of free time.We're all about to head over to the beach and walk Paul's dogs.Want to join us? I can come by and pick you up.

Rosario tapped her phone to her lip thoughtfully. With one exam down, she still had a pile of work to go, but her mood was bright from the success of the day and she quickly wrote out an agreement before she could second guess herself.

Soon, Rosario found herself buckling into the passenger seat of Michael's car. Taylor was in the back, talking animatedly over the quiet noise of the 'same' playlist going in the background. Rosario couldn't seem to keep a smile off her face as she listened, and every once in a while she could feel Michael's eyes slide over to her.

By the time they reach the beach, the sky is beginning to go pink with the sunset. Michael, Rosario, and Taylor all stopped by the stairs and waited for Paul and the others. They came a few minutes later, a big yellow golden retriever/yellow lab mix leading the way. The group exchanged hellos and hugs before taking off down the shoreline.

Rosario found herself looking through the sand, stooping down to pick up pieces of sea glass.The foggy green hue of a piece of glass in her hand engrossed her so much that she began to lag behind her friends. She didn't even realize how far behind she had fallen until there was a tap on her shoulder. Michael stood with her at the water's edge. He hung back from the water, his hand outstretched toward her.

Rosario opened her palm reflexively and he dropped in a handful of sea glass pieces.

"Thanks."

Michael smiled softly and it lit something up within her. His blue eyes were sparkling like the sea, more comforting than the smell of her mother frying up onions and garlic for arroz con pollo, and she was at home.

At that moment, there was no touch of gray within her. The gray had been receding for weeks -- whether it was due to therapy or the outdoors or anti-depressants, she didn't know. The elation struck so keenly that words bubbled up from her, and suddenly, she was speaking.

"Do you want to go to the Spring Formal with me?" she asked boldly.

Michael froze, his hand dropping. The shift in his posture was so sudden that on instinct Rosario stumbled back. The color of the sunset highlighted the ashen tone of Michael's face.

"I have to go." He said after a moment, his words barely audible over the sound of the waves.

"What?" Rosario panicked. For a second the disappointment is so dizzying that she can't tell if she wants to cry or throw up.

"I'll text Paul, let him to-to give you and Taylor a ride home. But I have to go, alright?" Michael fixed her with a pleading look before turning on his heel and sprinting up the beach back to where they came.

Rosario clenched the sea glass in her hand, fighting the urge to throw it into the ocean. Instead she sighed and, at the memory of Michael's fingers brushing hers, pocketed the collection to join the rest she had at home.

In a second of disassociation she pictured Michael running up the beach and bit back the urge to laugh. Of course things would turn out like this. Her joy had turned to pain, no gray to dull the sting of rejection.

Rosario stood at the shoreline and stared out at the horizon until she heard her friends again. She wasn't sure how long she'd been standing there, but judging from the furrowed brows of her friends she could tell that some time had passed.

"What happened to Michael?" Kathryn asks.

"Good question," Rosario said with a sigh. "You should definitely ask him the next time you see him. I'd love to know what he says."

"Are you kidding me?" Wade practically shouted as he leaned up into the forefront of the camera's view. "He did what?"

"Yup." Rosario popped the p with a smack and scooped a large helping of ice cream into her mouth.

"He...just ran away?" Kamala's response was measured, a contrast to Wade's outburst.

"What an asshole," Peter grouched.

"Right?!" Wade yelled. "I can't believe this guy. I thought he was alright when we met but, wow, does he need me to come down and talk some sense into him."

"Please don't," Rosario moaned and dropped her spoon with a clatter onto the top of her desk. "I am so humiliated. I can't deal with anyone talking about it ever again."

"Well that's not realistic." Kamala chided. "You're going to have to talk about it and get past it. I mean, you guys hang out all the time."

"Not anymore," Rosario whispered.

"What's that supposed to mean?" Peter asked.

"Ugh, I forgot how good your hearing is," Rosario sighed. "I just haven't really...responded to their texts since then?"

"Avoidance, great." Kamala raised an eyebrow judgmentally.

"Just for a while!" Rosario bargained. "Once this blows over, I'll go back to hanging out with them while awkwardly trying to avoid ever talking to Michael again."

"So...you just haven't responded to anything they've said for what, three days now?" Peter asked.

"Basically," Rosario admitted.

"Do you remember what happened the last time you just started ignoring everyone?" Kamala asked. "Remember how everyone thought something terrible happened?"

"Yeah, but this is different. This is--"

"Not to them it's not. To them this is just as scary as the first time. I'm sure they're worried about you. You should at least let them know you're okay, even if you don't explain everything," Kamala finished.

"Fine, fine." Rosario groaned and closed up her container of now-melted ice cream. So much for wallowing in her self-pity. "I'll let Taylor know. Happy?"

"Never," Peter said with a grin.

"Okay, goodbye now!" Wade waved at the camera. "You better hold up your end of things or I'll head over there and have a talk with them myself. And we all know how candid I like to be."

"Jeez, I get it." Rosario shook her head and hung up.

After a few moments of debate, she pulled out her cell phone. There was already an 'intimidating' text from Wade, urging her to talk to someone right now or he'd buy a bus ticket. Rosario opened a new text with Taylor, but before she could even begin to type out a message, somebody knocked at her door. She stilled, a small part of her brain wondering if Wade was really crazy enough to be here already when someone called from the door.

"Ro? It's me. Open up?"

"Taylor!" Rosario opened the door. "Come in; I was just about to text you."

"You were?" Taylor asked, sounding relieved. "I tried messaging you, but I never got a response, and then when I asked Michael if he was getting any messages from you he got all weird so I got worried and--"

Taylor broke off and considered Rosario.

Rosario had done her best to maintain a neutral expression at the mention of Michael, but judging from the look she was getting, she hadn't been successful.

Taylor narrowed her eyes. "What happened with you and Michael?"

"It's not a big deal, honestly," Rosario hedged as she sat down on her bed.

Taylor didn't respond.

Rosario patted the bed next to her, beckoning for Taylor to join her. Rosario hugged a pillow to her chest and took in a deep breath. "I asked Michael to go to the Spring Formal with me."

"Oh, Ro, that's great!" Taylor clapped, her eyes lighting up.

"He turned me down, Taylor." Rosario finished solemnly.

Her friend's face fell, hands still poised mid-clap. "He what?"

"Well, to be more accurate, he ran away and we haven't spoken since. I guess even a rejection would be better than what happened, huh?" Rosario laughed humorlessly.

Taylor glared off into the distance with a huff.

"Taylor?"

"That boy is so stupid!" Taylor spouted as she threw her hands into the air. "I can't believe he did that."

"Hey, it's not his fault." Rosario reached out to calm her friend down. "It's not the first time I asked him out and he shot me down. I bet he thought I'd outgrown it or something. It's my fault for not being able to move on. I should have--"

"Ro, stop it, please." Taylor clasped Rosario's hands in hers. "Don't undermine your feelings like this. I promise you, whatever you felt between you, it's--"

"No. Don't do that." Rosario stood and removed her hands from Taylor's. "Don't make up stuff for him. He's not here. You didn't see his *face*. I know how he feels about me now. I know it. I won't be stupid enough to make that mistake of seeing something that isn't there a third time, okay? I just need some time to get over myself and then things can go back to normal. I promise I can get there. I just need some time apart."

Taylor's gaze turned into something softer. "I get that you need time away from Michael, but can't we still spend time together?" She asked.

"Of course," Rosario assured her. "I'm sorry that by trying to cut Michael out I've cut you out as well. That's not fair to you. We can hang out just the two of us whenever you want. Well," she added, "after finals that is."

"Deal." Taylor laughed and stood up to hug her.

They spent a little while longer talking together in the middle of the dorm before Rosario had to leave for a study group. Taylor walked her down to the library before they parted ways with another hug. Before Rosario settled in to study, she made sure to text Wade and let him know she'd gone through with it and told someone what had happened. She didn't doubt that if she forgot to tell him, he'd be the next one knocking on her door.

CHAPTER ELEVEN

Rainbow -- Kesha

The rest of the semester rushed past in a blur

Rosario and Penelope still made their nightly walks around campus, sometimes stopping at the clearing, but most often parting ways near the library to meet with different study groups.

Rosario had her last meeting with Ford. He was happy enough to keep seeing her during the summer, but he believes she'd been doing well enough that they'd only need to meet once every other week. At the news, Rosario threw her arms around him in a big hug. He clapped her across the back once before ushering her out of the door, wishing her a good finals week.

As Rosario exited the building, she reached for her phone automatically drafting a text to Michael to let him know the good news, barely managing to stop herself from sending it. She deleted the message in its entirety before drafting a new message in the Friend Ship-- the group text between her, Wade, Peter, and Kamala.

Rosario: Guys! The therapy threat level has been downgraded from weekly to bi-weekly. Rejoice!

Wade: Doesn't that mean twice a week?

Peter: No, it means once every other week.

Kamala: Actually it can mean both.

Peter: Okay, but context clues you guys.

Rosario: Thank you for your excitement guys, I really appreciate it.

Peter: Yay Rosario! Congratulations!

Kamala: !!! <3 <3 <3

Wade: I still don't know if I should be celebrating here. It sounds like more therapy to me.

Peter: I want you all to know I just smacked Wade upside the head for you guys.

Wade: Congratulations Rosario!

He attached a gif of a puppy bouncing up and down with excitement.

Rosario: Thanks guys. Your genuine support means the world to me, always.

Wade: A *claps* N *claps* Y *claps* T *claps* I *claps* M *claps* E

Peter: You're not using that emoji correctly, Wade

Kamala: *claps*

Rosario was at breakfast when she received a strange text--a simple shot of Wade's tennis shoes on gray carpet.

Rosario: ?

Wade responded with another picture, this time of his shoes propped up on a desk.

Rosario: What are you doing?

Another picture. This one of a different pair of feet crossed on top of her familiar large knit comforter. Rosario jolted up straight before dumping her tray of food and rushing out back toward her dorm.

Sure enough, when she walked through the unlocked door she found Wade sprawled out on top of her bed, watching something on his phone.

"What are you doing here?" Rosario asked incredulously.

"We're here to take you to your dance!" Kamala answered, coming from just behind Rosario's shoulder.

"Holy crap!" Rosario yelped, heart thudding in her chest. "Where did you come from?"

"The closet," Peter replied, coming to stand next to them. "We couldn't all fit though, so Wade decided to be a little more obvious."

"I was never good about staying in the closet," he added, eyebrows waggling. Rosario snorted a laugh that was so gross sounding it made them all devolve into giggles for a few moments.

"You guys, you didn't have to come down here. Don't you have finals to be studying for?" Rosario said.

"Well, we can do that still too. We all brought work to do," replied Kamala.

"But we figured that since Michael was too dumb to realize a good thing when it came to him we could all jump on the opportunity to spend a magical night on the arm of a beautiful lady." Wade winked at her.

"You guys didn't have to do this, honestly," Rosario said. "I didn't even buy a ticket after everything that happened. I kind of just wanted to forget about it."

"C'mon Ro, it's us." Kamala looped an arm in hers. "I know you were secretly excited."

Rosario gave her a small smile, unable to tamp down the excitement she felt at being unexpectedly reunited with her friends.

"Okay, maybe I was a little bit excited. But--"

"Alright. We're here, we're excited, let's just do this, alright?" Peter encouraged.

"Alright," Rosario responded, pumping a fist in the air. "Let's do this."

——

That afternoon found them all at the local open air mall. It was a warm spring day out, and they all enjoyed the sun while moving from store to store, trying to find a dress for Rosario for that evening. Her friends had come prepared, but Rosario hadn't picked anything out after the disaster that was asking Michael out. She pushed aside the memory of his stricken face as she toured what the mall had to offer, instead trying to get swept up in her friends' conversation.

Peter and Wade were recounting a story of the surprise that Wade had tried to give Peter for their anniversary. Peter thought anniversaries were overrated, but Wade had tried to go all out. Somehow, that involved spiders. Despite listening to the story the whole time, somehow the spiders still didn't make any sense to her.

The story was just picking up to a conclusion when she spotted a dress she was instantly drawn to. It was midnight blue, strapless, with blue sequins on the bodice and a flowing tulle skirt.

"Wow, that's beautiful," Kamala said, voice filled with awe as she reached forward to run a hand down the fabric.

"You should try it on," Peter suggested.

"I don't know…" Sweat prickled at the back of Rosario's neck.

Shopping was always a gamble because things didn't always fit her. It would be humiliating to find out she didn't fit in the clothes at this store. But she cast one glance around at her friends--friends she'd known for years, friends who had dropped everything and traveled all this way to see her--and pulled the dress from the rack with a small bud of confidence. They'd support her no matter what.

A saleswoman led them back to the fitting rooms. Peter and Wade leaned against a wall while Kamala took a seat in front of a row of mirrors.

Rosario ducked into a room that had her name written on the door in a looping script. Once inside, she quickly stripped and pulled on the dress. It slid up with minimal effort and rested snugly against her. She beckoned Kamala to come and zip up the back. The bodice hugged her just right, tight enough to stay in place but not enough to be uncomfortable.

With a blush, Rosario walked out of the room to stand in front of the mirrors and take a turn in front of her friends.

"Woah, Ro, you look amazing," Peter said, mouth open.

"Honestly, it's true. That color looks fantastic on you," Kamala added.

"I'd definitely hit on you," Wade offered. "We'll take lots of pictures and put them online and tag Michael in them so he knows what he's missing out on."

Rosario shot him a glare.

Wade shrugged. "Okay, maybe I can be convinced not to do that last part. But you seriously look so beautiful. If I was straight and single--or bi and polyamorous--I'd be hitting on you."

Rosario swayed back and forth in front of the mirror, mesmerized by the shift of fabric and light glinting off the sparkly sequins on the top. Usually she felt weighted down by the softness of her belly and the heft of her arms, but something about this dress made her notice all the pretty parts of those things--her round belly was complemented by the ruching, and her large chest was lifted by the sweetheart neckline. Truly, she felt beautiful.

"I'm buying it," she decided.

Her friends cheered loudly enough that their saleswoman came back to give them a stern look.

"We're buying the dress, alright?" Wade said, leveling an equally serious stare. "No need to get all huffy."

Rosario bit her lip to keep a laugh at bay.

They checked out at the register, and spilled out into the sunny breezeway with laughter bubbling up between them. Rosario was all but floating on the feeling of having her friends around her. She couldn't help but think about Michael and wondered what he'd think of her dress, but with a shake of her head, she put the thought aside and focused on her friends, drawn into the moment. She realized Ford would have called that action *grounding* and she was happy that she could find mindfulness in this moment.

That night, they all went to Rosario's mother's house for dinner.

"It's nice to have you all around again," her mother said as she handed out heaping plates full of enchiladas, Mexican rice, refried beans, and corn. It was one of Peter's favorite meals, and her mother and Israel whipped it up just for the occasion. "It reminds me of the good old days, when you guys were still kids."

"I'm going to have to get this recipe from you," Kamala said as she shoveled a huge bite into her mouth.

"We'll just take home the leftovers," Wade said around a mouthful of food.

"Ay, you boys could learn something from Kamala. Everyone needs to know how to feed themselves."

"I know how to feed myself. It's called lunchables and frozen pizza," Wade said.

"Frozen pizza?" Israel wrinkled his nose. "You're like, super old. Shouldn't you know how to cook?"

Kamala snorted a laugh, choking on a piece of chicken. Rosario thumped her on the back.

"Wade and I the same age, you know," Rosario told her little brother.

"You heard me." Israel raised an eyebrow and took a measured bite of the enchiladas he had helped prepare.

After dinner, they all helped clear the table and wash the dishes. Rosario scrubbed at the sink, Kamala rinsed the dishes, Wade dried them, and Peter put them away. It was a familiar routine from their childhood and they fell into their roles without anything needing to be said. For a while after that they crowded around the TV, playing Mario Party with Israel and sending memes back and forth in the group chat, until Kamala declared she was tired and everyone agreed it was time for bed.

Peter and Wade claimed the fold out bed in the laundry room while Kamala went back to campus with Rosario to sleep in her dorm. They were a tight fit on the twin bed, but they wrapped themselves around one another and fell asleep warm and content.

CHAPTER TWELVE

Speechless -- Dan + Shay

The morning dawned bright and temperate. As Kamala and Rosario disentangled themselves, Penelope returned to the dorm, hair damp from her shower.

"Hey, are there any formal tickets left?" Rosario asked with a yawn.

"Oh man, no, it's all sold out." Penelope frowned. "I'm sorry."

"It's alright," Kamala said. "We can all just go out for a fancy dinner. I'll make the boys pay." She winked.

"Ha ha." Rosario nudged her friend in the side. "We can all pay for ourselves."

"Alright, if you say so…" Kamala shrugged.

Kamala took out her phone and called the boys, putting them on speakerphone while Rosario grabbed her laptop to research restaurant options.

"Ugh, no, why," Wade groaned as he answered the call.

"Good morning, sunshine!" Kamala called.

Rosario could almost hear their wince through the phone.

Kamala powered on. "The formal is sold out, so I told Rosario we'd take her on a hot date instead. We're looking up restaurants now."

"Sounds good," Peter hummed, still sounding mostly asleep. The group spent the next twenty minutes going over all the different 'fancy' restaurants in town before settling on a local restaurant called Fess Parker.

"Guys, I don't know, this place seems...fancy." Rosario felt awkward saying it, but her savings had dwindled during her time at school.

"We'll cover it, don't worry." Wade said. "We were planning on buying the tickets and stuff, so this is no big deal."

"We'll see if you feel that way when the bill comes," Rosario teased.

"Just make the reservation already," Wade complained. "I want to go back to bed."

Rosario slipped out of the room to make the reservation, and when she returned, she found Kamala chatting with Penelope.

"So I hear you guys have a super secret spot on campus," Kamala said as soon as Rosario walked back in.

"Huh?" Rosario blinked before her brain caught up. "Oh, it's not really a secret."

"Want to show me?" Kamala asked.

"Sure," Rosario agreed, "but let's get some breakfast first."

They made it down to the dining hall right as breakfast was wrapping up. Rosario served herself a bowl of oatmeal while Kamala grabbed a few breakfast tacos. Kamala led them to a table in the corner where they sat and ate in relative silence.

Afterward, Rosario walked with Kamala down the now familiar path to the clearing. It was a bright, warm day and as they stepped into the space Kamala spun around to get the full view of the place.

"It's so...peaceful," Kamala said. "You can't even hear the people on campus."

"It's even better at night," Rosario added. "Maybe after dinner we can all come back here."

"I don't know if Wade should be allowed, actually," Kamala said. "That boy is anything but peaceful."

Rosario laughed, and after a few minutes, they headed back to her dorm. Kamala and Rosario took turns showering before Wade and Peter came by the dorm to pick them up. They spent the day exploring Cost Village and by the time night fell, Rosario buzzed with anticipation. Something about getting all dressed up had always made her giddy. They all brought their clothes to Rosario's mom's house and shared space in the small bathroom getting ready. Kamala did Rosario's makeup and hair. Somehow, she turned her wiry mess of waves into luscious, shiny curls, and her eye makeup was smoky in a way that was subtle instead of the usual raccoon look Rosario accomplished when she tried on her own.

As she stepped out of the bathroom, the boys whooped and hollered at her look.

"Oh shit I'm bi as hell" Wade said, fanning himself.

"Thanks?" Rosario looked over at Peter, but he merely looped and arm around her shoulder, drawing her into a tight sideways hug.

"Oh, mija, you all look so wonderful!" Rosario's mother fawned over them, snapping a few pictures of them in front of the fireplace. Rosario rolled her eyes, but secretly she was pleased that her mother was so excited for them.

"One selfie before we hit the road," Wade declared. He stretched his arm out to get the whole group in the shot. The end result was priceless. Wade smacked a kiss on Peter's cheek, so Peter was blushing profusely behind his glasses while Kamala and Rosario pulled close, wide grins on their faces.

"Instant profile pic!" Kamala declared. The group agreed, each one changing their picture to the same thing.

"This is going to make commenting on each other's posts so confusing," Peter muttered. Wade snickered and elbowed him in the side.

"Just go along with it, peer pressure and all that."

They all piled into Wade' car and made the drive downtown to the restaurant. Wade sprung for valet parking and they walked into the glinting lobby with childlike wonder.

"Wow," Peter said, whistling. "This place is fancy."

"See, I told you guys, it's--"

As Rosario took a few steps into the lobby, her eyes fell on a familiar face. She stiffened, staring wide eyed at the person just a few feet away. Michael was standing in front of the restaurant, a small box in his hand, grinning at her sheepishly.

"Uhh…" She said, dumbstruck.

Kamala shoved her.

Rosario blinked and turned to find her friends fixing her with matching looks of mischief.

"Go!" Peter nudged her and Rosario stumbled forward before regaining composure. She came to a halt in front of Michael. He looked stunning, like the main love interest in every Korean drama she had recommended to Taylor. His hair was artfully arranged with honest to go product holding in it place, he had a sleek blazer on over a button up that had tiny polka dots all over it. Upon further inspection Rosario noticed they were actually pokeballs. Her heart flipped in her chest at the sight. He was such a nerd and she was in so much trouble.

"Hey," he began.

"Hi," Rosario managed, disbelieving. "What are you doing here?"

Michael rubbed a hand on the back of his neck and his eyes drank her in from head to toe.

"Do you mind if we talk somewhere a little more private?" He asked, bouncing his gaze to her friends.

Rosario turned to find them all staring intently at them. Once they realized she had seen them, Kamala grabbed the boys by the arms and forcefully steered them away. Rosario bit back a laugh before gesturing for Michael to follow her outside.

Fairy lights lined a small rose garden to the side of the hotel entrance. They took a seat on a bench partially hidden from the main doors. At first Michael sat at the opposite end of the bench, but after a moment he slid close enough that Rosario could smell the spicy scent of his cologne and minty fresh breath.

"So…" Rosario prompted.

"So." Michael rubbed his hands on his pants before he looked up at her and gave her a small, nervous smile. "I wanted to apologize for leaving things like I did the other day."

A flush of mortification inched up Rosario's face at the memory of his shocked expression and quick retreat.

"I had been...struggling. With what I feel. For a while…" Michael paused again."And then you just...came out and said it, so easily. I freaked out--"

"It wasn't easy," Rosario said. "Not really. I was just so happy, I--"

"I know, and I just stomped all over that." Michael shifted to face her fully. "I don't know how to tell you how sorry I am. I…" He paused before closing his eyes and sighing deeply. "I -- I have an anxiety...issue."

Rosario didn't know what she expected to hear, but it wasn't that.

"And it holds me back sometimes. My past relationships have been... rocky. I just...don't know where to go from here. It feels like there's so much on the line. Your relationship with our friends could get messed up, plus I'm so much older than you, I don't think--"

Rosario rested her hand on Michael's shoulder. The touch made him pause.

"I know there's a lot to consider," Rosario began, "but I also know the anxiety brain has a way of making things seem worse than they are."

Michael nodded and ran a hand through his hair, completely messing up everything he had finessed into place.

"I need you to know that I've got stuff too though. These past few months have been really tough because...because I've been depressed," she said in a rush, breathing in deep. "And I don't know what to do with that, not really. I've been working hard to move past it, but it isn't the first time something like this has happened. And maybe it'll happen again. I know that I let things suffer because of it, including my relationship with you.".

"I guess we both have our own stuff, huh?" he said finally.

"Yeah, definitely." Rosario let her hand drift to his forearm. "But where does that leave us?"

Silence fell.

"I don't want to pass up happiness just because I'm scared," Michael whispered.

"And I don't want to let this gray ruin another part of my life," Rosario added. "I've still got a lot of things to work on--"

"So do I," Michael added. "That doesn't mean we can't be happy together."

Rosario squeezed his forearm once before letting her hand drop back to her lap.

"I don't know about you," Rosario began, "but I am starving."

Michael nodded his head and laughed.

"I could stand to eat." Michael stood and offered his hand to Rosario.

She took it gratefully as always, loving the feel of his guitar-calloused hand in hers. This time, Michael didn't drop her hand. Instead, he laced their fingers together, rubbed the pad of his thumb across the back of her hand, and guided them inside.

Her friends' eyes tracked to where her hand was linked in Michael's and their expressions lit up. She was in for some serious teasing when they were on their own.

"Are you doing this now?" Wade asked when they approached, garnering a swift elbow to the gut from Kamala. "I mean, are we doing this now? Eating? Are we?"

"Yeah," Rosario said. "Let's go inside."

They filed into the restaurant to a table in the middle of the room. Once they were seated, they began bickering animatedly over the menu. Rosario ended up getting a simple pasta dish while Michael got a salad. Wade on the other hand went for the impressive surf and turf on the menu, which Peter declared he'd split with him.

"Aww what?" Wade whined. "I wanted to stuff myself."

"Poor baby," Peter patted him on the head. "You'll have to settle for actually enjoying your food for once."

Kamala laughed, nearly snorting her gulp of water, and Rosario thumped her on the back.

"I'm fine," Kamala said, voice rough.

"You sure? I could hit you, just to be safe," Wade said, making a motion to stand up. Peter pulled him down with a jolt, and Wade pouted.

Their waitress brought their dinners out to them and they eagerly began to eat.

"So, Michael," Wade began around a mouthful of mashed potatoes, "Want to hear about the time Rosario decided to cut her own bangs?"

"OH no, we're not telling that story!" Rosario replied, setting down her fork to glare at Wade.

"They were about an inch long by the time she was done, I think?" Kamala chimed in. Rosario groaned and took an extra big gulp of seltzer water to hide her embarrassment.

"That's nothing," Michael assured her. "One time I bleached my own hair, and almost ended up bald." Rosario snorted a laugh, nearly making water go up her nose. The chatter continued on, telling story after story, until all the entrees were long gone. After a dessert of creme brulee was cleared away they left the restaurant together.

"So I know you mentioned that the tickets to the formal were all sold out," Michael said, "but speaking as someone who has been to this formal -- we can sneak in."

"Really?" Wade grinned. "Tell me more."

"Just follow me," Michael said, sticking his thumb out toward his car.

Rosario hesitated, looking over to her friends for permission to ride with him. Kamala shoved her in the right direction, and with that, Rosario jogged after him. Michael held open the car door, and once she slid inside, she queued up the "same" playlist. The soft tones of "Anything for You" by Ludo reverberated in the small space between them. As they drove, they sang along, but then Michael reached over and turned down the volume.

"I made this playlist for you, you know," he said, taking a hand from the wheel to run his fingers through his hair.

"What do you mean?" she asked.

"These are all the songs we have in common. I figured this would be just about the perfect playlist for you."

Rosario looked at him incredulously. "Are you serious?"

"Yeah," he confessed, gluing his eyes to the road. "Is that weird? I'm sorry if that's weird, I just--"

In response, Rosario cranked up the volume and began singing at the top of her lungs

"I've picked up rocks from distant moons astronomers will discover soon, but I would give them all back just for you!"

Michael cast a surprised look her way and threw his head back to laugh. He joined, his volume more reasonable than hers, and they sang together all the way to the beach.

The formal took place at a beach side hotel. They parked by the sand and Wade, Peter, and Kamala joined them by Michael's car, and he debriefed them.

"The ballroom is open to the beach. All we have to do is walk in through the sands and go in the beach entrance and we can sneak in. We're dressed up enough that no one will notice us."

Michael winked and began humming the 007 theme before turning to make his way across the sand. Rosario stooped to remove her heels, unwilling to let her clumsiness ruin the night. She held them in her hand as she picked her way across the sand. Kamala wrapped an arm around her, while Wade and Peter hung back and whispered to each other, barely audible over the sound of the waves.

"So...things seem to be going alright," Kamala prodded, her voice soft in the night air.

"Mmhm," Rosario hummed, casting a nervous glance toward Michael's back where he led the group. He had removed his blazer and all she could see was tiny pokeballs spanning the spread of his broad shoulders. He moved forward purposefully and didn't seem to be listening. "But we definitely need to talk later about how you planned all of this."

"What are you talking about?" Kamala asked innocently. "Are you talking about the fact that Michael reached out to us and asked us if he could elbow into our date night with you? And how Wade and Peter and I made sure he had *quite* the stern talking to before he could do any of this? Is that what you're talking about?"

"Oh my god," Rosario groaned. "I am so going to kill you."

Kamala threw back her head and laughed, causing Michael to give them an odd stare. Rosario grinned back at him.

Michael stopped a few feet away from a gated entrance to a patio that was surrounded with strings of fairy lights. A DJ played music from the front of the area and a large group of people danced together on the floor. Tables filled the edges of the dance floor, some with people already eating desserts or having the required non-alcoholic drinks. Michael walked up to the gate and opened it, letting Rosario and Kamala in before swinging it shut on Wade and Peter. They stopped short and glared up at Michael who grinned. There was a tense moment before Wade huffed and laughed loud enough to draw attention to them.

"Oh man, you've gone and done it," Wade said. "I promised them I'd be on my best behavior, but you've gone and drawn first blood. When you look back and wonder how it all got this far I want you to think about this moment and know it was your own doing that brought us here."

"Whoa," Peter said as he clapped a hand on his boyfriend's shoulder. "What I think Wade here is trying to say is you're gonna fit in just fine with us."

"Now *that* should worry you," Kamala said.

Michael kicked the gate back open for the boys and they all made their way inside. Rosario set her shoes down on a table and let her friends drag her to the dance floor.

She turned to pull Michael in with them, only to find him hovering at the edge of the crowd, fidgeting in a way that betrayed his nervousness. Rosario broke away from her friends and held out her hand. He gave her a small, worried smile before allowing her to guide him out onto the dance floor.

The song was fast and easy to dance to. Rosario let the music guide her and watched as Michael slowly began to unwind. Between Kamala's practiced moves, Peter's awkward side to side slide, and Wade's ridiculous grinding, Michael's nervous shuffles melted into something more relaxed. They spent song after song on the floor, calling out to one another as they danced, until Penelope sidled up to them. Rosario thought they looked like quite the pair--Ro in blues and silvers, Penelope in a bright pink crop and tulle skirt with sparkly black combat boots.

"Hey!" she yelled over the noise.

"Penelope!" Rosario pulled her friend into a hug. "Oh my god, hi!"

"Hi," Penelope began. "I kind of thought you mentioned you didn't get tickets to this."

"Uhhh..." Rosario paused and looked around at her friends. "Surprise?"

"I'm not going to tell you to leave," Penelope said, and Rosario's shoulders drooped with relief. "I'm just surprised to see you guys here. All...of you guys." Her eyes flicking to Michael as her brows lift suggestively.

"Me too," Rosario replied, unable to tamp her giddiness down. Penelope stuck with them for a few songs, dancing between Peter and Wade, before Rosario ended up tugging Michael from the dance floor.

"What's up?" he asked.

"Just need a break," she said.

"Then let's take a walk," Michael offered.

He took her by the hand and led her back out onto the beach, Rosario taking the moment to wiggle her toes into the white sand. They wandered away from the hotel until the sounds of the party grew distant, quieted by the darkness of the night. It was too dark to search for sea glass, but Michael still guided them to the edge of the water. He planted Rosario at the edge of the waves and stood behind her, wrapping her in his arms from behind. The water lapped at her feet and she sighed, breathing in a lungful of crisp, salty sea air. As she tipped her head back to look at the stars, Michael peered down at her and gave her a mischievous smile before he pressed a soft kiss to her forehead. Rosario blushed softly under the starlight, her happiness radiating without any hint of gray.

CHAPTER THIRTEEN

Save Myself -- Ashe

Going back to Mooreland always felt like putting on a piece of clothing that just doesn't fit anymore. She still loved it, but nothing sat right and in the end it just made her sad.

But, regardless, it was her grandmother's eightieth birthday and that was a big enough deal to draw in family members from Mexico, so the least she can do is drive two hours and live through a few days of introvert hell.

"Make sure to bring your boyfriend!" her grandmother said each time she'd spoken with Rosario about the party. Each time, Rosario blushed and agreed that she would bring Michael along so that they could meet in person.

Michael, for his part, seemed to be excited enough for everyone. He pulled up at Rosario's house wearing black Ray Bans, his hair styled perfectly, a wide grin on his face--it was enough to make Rosario want to tug him down into a kiss right on the spot, but she paused. The newness of their relationship was still taking some getting used to. She didn't know how to maneuver in their unfamiliar settings.

Michael must have sensed her hesitance because he tipped his sunglasses down the bridge of his nose enough to let Rosario see his bright blue eyes and the laughter that was there before leaning down to press a soft kiss to the tip of her nose. Rosario sputtered, caught off guard, which made Michael lean back and laugh.

"You about ready to head out?" he asked.

Rosario's mother had made the trip down with Israel a few days ago to begin prepping the food and getting the house ready.

Michael had agreed to take Rosario down, since they were only staying for one night. Michael arrived at her mother's townhouse just after seven in the morning, and she was not chipper enough to be dealing with his antics.

"I need like a million more cups of coffee," she muttered as she let him inside.

"We'll stop at Summermoon on the way out of town, I promise." Michael followed her into her laundry room slash bedroom where clothes spilled out of a small rolling suitcase painted to look like a giant comic strip.

"Do you need help closing that up?" he asked.

"Oh, what?" Rosario responded distractedly. "No, I've got it."

She rifled through a box on her desk before making a frustrated noise and upending the box on the floor.

"Whoa," Michael commented. "That got serious."

"Not really," Rosario said with a note of triumph in her voice as she snagged up a silver locket from the mess and pocketed it before bending down to scoop everything back where it came. Michael stooped down to help her and in a moment the room was right once again. Rosario shoved her things inside the suitcase one by one until finally she leaned on the top of the bag to zip it up. Michael watched as she struggled and hovered like he wanted to help.

With a final grunt, the zipper slid home.

"See, told you I didn't need any help."

Michael rolled his eyes behind the sunglasses.

"I definitely saw that," she told him as she stood the suitcase up and began to drag it outside.

"Can I at least roll that thing for you?" Michael asked. Rosario shot him an appraising look over her shoulder before handing over the bag.

"I need to grab my purse from upstairs," Rosario said. "Will you please go put this away and wait for me by the car?"

"Sure thing," Michael agreed.

Rosario watched him walk all the way to his trunk before she closed the front door and sprinted up the stairs. She caught her foot on the edge of the last one and fell with a slam and a whimper.

Unfazed, she went for her phone and dialed the second number on her speed dial.

"City morgue, you stab 'em we slab 'em," Wade's voice droned.

"Ugh, Wade, no, c'mon," Rosario groaned and thumped her head against the railing of the stair. "Where's Kamala?"

"Right here!" a familiar voice called from the background. "We're baking a cake for your abuela."

"Oh no." Rosario thumped her head again.

"Don't worry, Wade isn't allowed in the kitchen," Peter chimed in.

"I'm in a supervisory role," Wade drawled. "So you're kind of talking to the boss. And as the boss my time is incredibly valuable, what can I do for you? And make it quick!"

"Michael is here." Rosario whispered. "I'm freaking out."

A chorus of cat calls went up from the other line before Wade spoke again.

"Why are you freaking out? You have the condoms I gave you, right?"

"Yes, Wade, I have the condoms you gave me when I turned eighteen. And the condoms you gave me when I went off to college. And the condoms you gave me when I told you about Michael. AND I also have the condoms you gave me when Michael and I started dating."

"One, please don't tell me you're bringing all of that. Your luggage will be huge." -- Rosario heard a snort of laughter -- "Second, some of those might need to be thrown away. They do have expiration dates, you know."

"Yes, and three, no one needs that many condoms," Rosario hissed into the phone, becoming increasingly aware of the fact that Michael was probably wondering what was taking so long.

"Well I mean if you're not going to use them Peter and I---ow!" After a beat of silence, Wade whined, "My boyfriend just threw a spatula at me and it hit me in the eye."

Kamala cackled.

"Guys, focus! Michael is going to be meeting my whole family in a few hours." Rosario took a deep breath and tried to call to mind all her anxiety stemming tricks she'd worked on with Ford.

"Everyone loves Michael, all right?" Kamala sounded closer now, her voice loud over the background sound of Peter and Wade bickering. "And everyone loves you. And your family is super nice. You don't need to worry."

"Plus we'll be there!" Wade yelled.

"Yeah, Wade will be there. He's a lightning rod for hate. Michael will be fine." Peter proclaimed before letting out a choked grunt.

"Boys, stop hitting each other," Kamala chided. "Ro, we'll all be together in a few hours. Until then, just enjoy some solo time with your man, okay?"

"Fine," Rosario sighed. "I'll see you guys soon."

She hung up and sprinted into the living room to pick up her purse and keys before descending the stairs slowly only to rush out the door, nearly forgetting to lock it in her haste.

"Everything all right?" Michael asked once she'd gotten into the car.

"Fine, yeah, everything's fine." Rosario buckled in.

As Michael pulled away from the curb, Rosario did her best to practice her deep breathing discreetly. He had the radio set to NPR and the news about the political unrest in the country wasn't doing much to help her pulse regulate. She reached out and pressed a random button, shifting the radio from news to top forty hits.

Rosario used the short drive to the coffee shop as a window of time to focus on reining in her mounting anxiety. She slipped the locket out of her pocket and opened it, lifting it to her nose. It was a small aromatherapy diffuser that Penelope gifted her.

Ford told Rosario about grounding scents, she'd anxiously shared the knowledge with Penelope and together they worked toward developing a blend of essential oils that was soothing enough to calm her nerves while still being sharp enough to snap her out of anxiety. The current concoction was a mix of spearmint and eucalyptus.

By the time they had pulled into their parking spot down the road, Rosario was breathing normally, the scent still lingering. Summermoon was a quaint little mom and pop establishment with an honest to goodness white picket fence around it and adirondack chairs spread across it's spacious front porch. They went up to the outdoor counter and ordered.

"I'll take a hot chocolate, a peanut butter and jelly wrap, a moon milk latte, and two breakfast tacos."

Rosario shot in ahead of him and slammed down her card on the countertop. "And I'll be paying for that, thank you very much."

Michael rolled his eyes and gave in while the barista rang them up, looking suitably unimpressed.

"I would have let you split it with me, you know," Michael said as they walked over to the bar to wait for their food.

"Really? I kind of took you for one of those 'the man has to do everything' kind of guys."

"Wow, really?" Michael laughed. "No way. I'm all about fairness, sweetheart." He winked at her and the term of endearment made her shiver.

"Okay, well, next time you get to cover it."

"Good." Michael scooped up their food in his hand and his cup in the other and they went o to sit down and eat their breakfast. Rosario was halfway through her first breakfast taco before she spoke.

"Want some of my coffee?"

"No," Michael smiled around the rim of his cup. "You ask me that every time."

"It's good!" Rosario lifted the cup to his face. "Come on, just a sip. I haven't even had any yet, no cooties."

"I actually don't drink coffee. Though I'm sure this place has good stuff, it smells amazing."

"You don't...drink...coffee?" Rosario sputtered, horrified. "How do you live?"

Michael threw his head back and laughed. "I get by."

"What about energy drinks?"

"Nope."

"Tea?"

"Nu-uh."

"Are you Mormon?" Rosario blurted out.

"What?" Michael gave her a strange look. "Ro, we go to the same church."

"I know I just...I mean...nothing?"

"I like hot chocolate?" He offered, lifting his cup. "You should try it, it's pretty great. Though, mine does have cooties."

Rosario took his drink and tipped it back. Michael watched, his face heating into a blush as her lips landed where his had just been. The warm, rich chocolate taste exploded over her tongue and ran warm down her throat.

"Woah, that is pretty good." Rosario agreed.

Their fingers met when she passed Michael his cup, and the touch sent a shiver down her spine. These fleeting touches still managed to move her even though they shared them all the time now.

Rosario took another bite of her food to keep her mouth and hands busy--nothing that could show how desperately she wanted more from him.

They finished their food in silence before Michael led them back to his car. Once they settled, he handed Rosario his phone and she queued up their playlist without even thinking. The music had changed in the time they'd been dating -- they both added songs they thought the other might like. It now sounded like a mix of two individuals rather than the tastes of one trying to fit another. It was jarring at times, but overall it was still her favorite playlist. That is, until--

"No, no, whyyy!" Rosario reached out toward the phone on the dashboard.

"No way, this is a great song." Michael batted her hand away.

"It is not. This was cool for like a month when I was eleven," Rosario groaned. But then she heard it, and it was too late, the song was latching into her head, ready to be stuck there for days.

Dog goes woof, cat goes meow, birds go tweet and mouse goes squeak, cow goes moo, frogs go croak, and the elephant goes toot--

Michael turned up the volume and sang.

"Ducks say quack, fish goes blub, and the seal goes ow ow ow," He waggled his eyebrows at Rosario.

Gave him a cheesy grin before jumping in.

"But there's one sound that no one knows....WHAT DOES THE FOX SAY!"

And that was how the rest of the two hour car ride went.

Mooreland had always been a dusty mess. When they rolled in the sun was reaching its peak height and baking the dirt in the streets. They pulled up outside of a white stucco house with green shutters in a neighborhood full of small houses on wide lots.

"This is it," Rosario said. "Your last chance to back out."

"Never." Michael looped and arm around her. Rosario squared her shoulders before walking up to the front door with him by her side. She rapped hard on the door three times, only to hear a shout from inside.

"Who the hell is knocking on my door?" The door swung open to reveal a short, smiling Mexican woman with thin silvering hair. "Because I know my nieta knows that this is her home and you don't need to knock when you enter your own home."

"Abuela," Rosario wrapped her abuela up into a strong hug, "I'm so happy to see you. Happy birthday!"

"Gracias, mija, gracias," her abuela said, squeezing her again before letting go and stepping back. She moved back a few feet and then gave Michael a critical once over. "Now who is this young man?"

"Abuela, this is Michael," Rosario darted a quick glance to her side but Michael was already moving forward.

"My name is Michael Lundgren. I'm Rosario's boyfriend." He fixed her abuela with what Rosario knew was his most winning smile and she could see the cogs turn in her grandmother's head.

"Mija, you didn't tell me he was so tall," she stage-whispered. "There's not enough room for those legs under the table!" She opened her arms wide and Michael took the opening to lean down and give her a hug. Over his shoulder, she continued, "That just means he'll have to play footsie with you all night."

"Ay, suegra, don't say that!" Rosario's mother called as she rounded the corner. She slapped Rosario's grandmother on the shoulder with a dish towel, causing her abuela to finally let go of Michael.

There was a hint of pink on Michael's cheeks that made Rosario smile.

"Hello mija." Her mother gave her a quick hug before moving on to Michael. "Thank you so much for taking care of my daughter. You have no idea how glad I am to have you here with us." She patted him on the shoulder.

"I'm sure my son would have loved to see this day," her abuela added.

"Are you kidding? He would have hated this," Rosario said with a grin. "He'd have been all shotguns and curfews."

"You're probably right," Rosario's grandmother said. "I know he'd get a kick out of seeing that Peter all grown up too. I hear he's got an internship with the LA Times."

"He hasn't stopped talking about it in weeks," answered Rosario. "He should be here any minute, you can hear all about it then."

"What can I do to help?" Michael asked Rosario's mother.

"Oh, bless you!" Rosario's mother exclaimed, leading him into the house.

"You're going to regret saying that!" Rosario hollered after them. Michael turned and waved as Rosario's mother brought outside.

Rosario followed her grandmother into the kitchen to make some masa for tortillas, and from the kitchen window, she could see Michael balancing on a ladder with a string of lights in his hands.

"Uh-oh, she's making him hang the lights."

"Well he's the tallest one, it makes sense." Her abuela began measuring out flour with her hands. "It wouldn't do to have a repeat of the time Wade got stuck up on one of the branches."

"Yeah, Kamala still brags about saving him." Rosario mixed the baking powder into the mound of flour. Her grandmother streamed questions that Rosario answered until they had an arsenal of little balls of dough lined up for cooking.

Rosario was cleaning her hands off on her apron when a knock came from the front door. A moment later, Peter, Wade, and Kamala rushed in, arms full of tupperware.

"Ninos!" Rosario's grandmother pulled them in. "It's so good to see you."

"You too, abuela," Kamala said. "Now where can we put these presents?"

"They're food presents, so decide now if you want to share or not," Wade waved around a box in the air.

"Are those the cookies with the marshmallows in them?" Abuela asked.

"We made two boxes, just in case you want to keep one for yourself" Peter held out a second box.

"I always knew you were a smart one," Abuela told him. "That's probably what landed you that internship I've heard so much about."

"Oh, what internship?" Kamala asked, feigning ignorance.

"I don't know, Kamala. Why didn't Peter mention this internship?" Wade exaggerated a face of surprise.

Peter ignored them. "Let me tell you all about it, abuela--"

By four in the afternoon, over sixty people are crowded the back yard with more still on the way. The neighborhood streets burst with cars parked along the sidewalks and on the lawn.

In any other neighborhood, the neighbors would be complaining or calling the cops, but everyone in this area had lived in these houses together for over twenty years. Every was in attendance, bringing trays of food and coolers of drinks and staking out their own corner of the lawn. One of Rosario's primos gifted her abuela a serious bluetooth speaker system, currently streaming music. A makeshift dancing area opened up in the center of the backyard where groups of people doing the cumbia, holding sweating bottles of beer in their hands. Peter and Wade were cutting up the dancefloor, but Wade was doing his grinding thing again much to her abuela's amusement.

Rosario's younger cousin Hannah had Michael's hand in hers and was painting his fingernails with imaginary nail polish.

"I think they look great." Michael stretched out a hand to examine her handiwork. "How long do I need to let them dry?"

"Oh no, they're done right away" Hannah patted him on the leg and said, "It's not real nail polish," before dashing away to play with someone else. Rosario chuckled and elbowed Michael who shrugged and tugged her closer to his side.

"Am I a bad person if I say I need a break?" he asked, his voice barely a whisper.

"No, of course not!" Rosario cupped the side of his face. "Let's go get some air."

Michael followed her back into the house. As they entered, they nearly ran face first into Rosario's mother whose arms were loaded down with a platter of food that Michael took from her to keep from toppling over.

"Mom," Rosario began, steadying her on her feet. "We were just, uh, going to--"

"If you're going somewhere, would you mind getting more ice?" Her mother asked, taking the platter back from Michael.

"Sure, ice, yeah." Rosario watched as her mother rushed past.

The street outside still carried the loud noise of music and chatter toward them as they got into Michael's car. They've turned off the street when Michael finally said, "You know they definitely think we ran off to have sex."

Rosario flinched and a wave of blood rushed to her face.

"Oh no," she groaned.

"That's not the best reaction I've ever had when discussing sex with someone I'm dating, but it's also surprisingly not the worst--"

"What? Oh, no, I'm sorry." Rosario laughed despite herself. "I'm just sure my family will get to talking. You know how family can be."

"Not really," Michael said. "Not like this. You've met my family, Ro. We're small, and quiet, and we love each other and it's great, but this is totally different." He glued his eyes to the road, but a gentle awe filled his voice. "You guys take everyone in around you. Peter, Wade, Kamala, me--everyone was so welcoming and nice. They ribbed me and put me to work, just like family. They make anyone feel like family."

"Yeah..." Rosario looked out the window.

"Hello ma'am," Richard said. "My name is Richard Roman and I'm dating your daughter." He extended his hand and instead wound up in Rosario's mother's arms.

She squeezed him and Richard went rigid. As Rosario's mother let go, Israel wrapped himself around Richard's legs.

"That's my little brother," Rosario said. They crowded the doorway, eager to get the first look at Richard.

The rest of her family was already out in her abuela's back yard. Every year Rosario celebrated her birthday with a barbecue at her grandmother's house, but this year was the first year she'd decided to bring a significant other.

Eventually Richard worked himself free and came inside to give Rosario a deep kiss on the lips. She pulled away, ducking her head away from view.

"She's always been shy," Rosario's mother stated.

"We've been trying to work on that," Richard said. "Your home is lovely, by the way."

"I'm happy to hear it," Rosario's abuela hollered. "And who are you?"

"I"m Richard, ma'am," he reached out, and she gave him a firm handshake.

"Richard, wonderful. Do you think you could give me a hand and help me wipe down some dishes?"

"Uh..." He gave Rosario a panicked look, but she waved him on. "Sure."

Rosario's grandmother tugged him into the kitchen where all she could hear was the sound of plates clinking and the faucet running.

Rosario, meanwhile, joined her friends outside, while Wade, Peter, and Kamala lined up cups near the drink table.

As they worked, Richard stormed out of the house, a large wet spot clear on his pants. Wade coughed out a loud laugh before Peter slapped a hand over his boyfriend's mouth.

"What happened?" Kamala asked.

"That sink is what happened. It's so old it kept getting water everywhere! And then this happened and your grandmother laughed at me, Rosie. She laughed."

"I laughed too," Wade said, and Peter slapped a hand over his mouth again.

"Whatever." Richard wrung out his hands in frustration before grabbing for Rosario and pulling her aside. "I need to go home and change."

"What?" Rosario asked. "Now? We're going to eat soon."

"I can't eat like this!" He gestured to his pants and Rosario bit back a laugh.

Damn it, Wade.

"It'll be okay. It's hot outside. It'll dry off in a few minutes," she assured him.

"No, I look ridiculous. I'm not staying." Richard took a step back, the space between them cooling.

"Are you at least coming back?" Rosario asked, anger edging into her voice.

"Rosario, honestly, do you even want me here? This seems more like a family thing."

"Of course I want you here!" Rosario said, fighting to keep her volume down. "My other friends are here too, so it's not really a family thing--"

"Right, about that." Richard crossed his arms. "You've spent all your time with them since I've been here. We've hardly said two words to each other."

"You've been in the kitchen, I was--"

"You could have been helping me, Rosie, instead of leaving me to this." He gestured to his clothes again.

"So this is my fault somehow?".

"Hey, guys." Peter popped his head up from behind Richard's back. "You're kind of drawing some attention. I think the guest room is open if you need to--"

Richard pushed past Peter, toward the front door. Rosario watched as he stormed to his car. Kamala came to stand by her as he drove off.

Rosario didn't get a text from him until the middle of dinner.

Richard: I'm sorry I made a scene. i hope you have a great birthday.

Rosario began typing out a response, only to delete it and close the messaging app.

Richard: I said I'm sorry. I can make it up to you. What else do you want?

Rosario: If you left now you'd definitely make it in time for dessert. You could even see Peter trying to learn to dance. It's going to be great.

Richard: I can't come back after that.

Rosario: I promise you no one will say anything

A few minutes passed Rosario kept the phone out in front of her at the table, anxious until the screen lit up again.

Richard: I bought tickets to a midnight movie. Let me know when you're back at home so I can go pick you up.

A million thoughts rushed to her head--I'm not going home before midnight, why didn't you ask me, why didn't you just come, don't you care what I--

Rosario: Alright. See you then. I love you

Richard: You too.

Michael drove them around before Rosario decided to tell him where to go. The trip had been more about getting out rather than going somewhere. They brought the ice, and the party was even louder than when they left it, coolers now empty and kids full of cake. Michael ended up playing guitar for all the kids on an old acoustic their neighbor tia Lisa had in her garage. Rosario dances with Israel to goofy to the goofy pop songs Michael sings until the grass cools under her feet and it's nearing ten o'clock.

The food had been divided up into to-go plates long ago, and many a tia had come in to help clean up the dishes. Now the house felt empty and as they waved abuela off to bed A wave of sadness washed over Rosario at the thought of saying goodbye to this place again.

"There's still time to go do something all together," Peter said, obviously trying to lead the group to an after party.

"Yeah, maybe a movie?" Kamala added.

"I do love movies," Michael said with a grin. He gave Rosario a considerate look before she smiled and nodded. "Alright, movies it is."

They met up in the city center where the biggest movie theater was for some late night showing of an action film. No one bought snacks, but somehow Wade ended up getting popcorn in Kamala's hair and by the end of the movie they are all cracking jokes about things that aren't supposed to be funny. They filed out of the theater and into the cooling summer air, and Rosario was simply happy.

In the end, Rosario's anxiety had been inadequate. It had come up with hundreds of scenarios of how Richard could come back into her life after the church fiasco, but this encounter was almost too cliche to bear. Here they were, standing in the cold late night air after their movie and walking towards them, arm in arm with some (petite, beautiful, and seemingly young) girl, was Richard. Rosario had only noticed him because he was waving at them, a smile on his face.

"Ro!" He called, "Is that you?"

"You've got to be kidding me." Wade said, "Why is this waste of space talking to us?" He wasn't making any effort to lower his voice, and Richard raised an eyebrow as he approached.

"Now now, let's all be nice. Wouldn't want to make a bad impression on my friend here, would you?" Richard gestured toward the girl who giggled and squeezed Richard's arm.

"Hey, my name is Melissa," the girl introduced herself with a warm smile. "How do you know Richard?"

"Oh boy," Peter muttered.

"Well, Melissa, this is a lovely segue into why you should run as far from this man as possible," Wade reached out as if to untangle the couple's entwined limbs but Richard deftly maneuvered so that Wade was instead giving him an awkward handshake.

"Wade is so funny, he's always joking around," Richard said. "Isn't that right, Rosie?"

Ro blinked. Everything had unfolded so fast, and was so starkly different from the night she just had, that words failed her for a moment. Then, so gently she thought she had imagined it, Ro felt a light pressure around her wrist. Michael. She glanced up and saw him looking at her reassuringly.

"Actually Melissa, Richard and I used to date."

"Oh." Melissa gripped Richard's arm tighter and gave Ro a withering stare. "Well, I think we should be going—"

"Wait, Melissa, just a sec." Ro stepped forward, causing Melissa to take a reflexive step back. "I just want to tell you—"

"Now now, Rosie, think before you speak." Richard's tone was condescending and it made Rosario's face flush.

"Oh, I'm done thinking. It's time to speak." Rosario glared up at Richard, who seemed to be viewing this moment with glee. "Melissa, Richard is a giant gaslighting asshole who abused me the entire time we were together. He manipulated me and isolated me and when I finally left he still haunted me. Wade was right, you should run."

A beat of silence passed before Richard scoffed.

"Really, this is just sad. I knew you resented me for moving on, but I didn't think you'd be so petty as to try and ruin my future relationships" Richard sighed and looked at Melissa before shrugging as if to say 'what will these people say next'.

A hot flash of embarrassment rushed through Rosario. Of course she sounded crazy, Richard was an expert at getting people to be on his side. Her brain began to spiral down a well of anxiety, but then something happened that truly surprised her. Clarity came to her in the form of her therapist's calm voice, telling her to breathe in deep and recognize five things she could see. Richard was still talking, but Ro breathed in the crisp evening air and counted—tree, light pole, Wade, Peter, Kamala. Four things she could touch. Michael, the ring on her finger, the chipped nail polish on her thumb, the soft fabric of her favorite hoodie. Three things she could hear—Richard droning on and on, the soft whoosh of distant traffic, music from a car parked nearby. Rosario took another deep breath. She didn't need two or one.

"Believe me or not, that's up to you," Rosario focused her attention on Richard. She looked into his eyes and saw the glee of a predator about to pounce. But she was not afraid. "Richard, I will never forgive you for the way you treated me. The things you did to me. That you took from me. I am moving on, but you don't get my forgiveness. You did awful, terrible things, but I'm done letting them hold me back." Rosario closed her eyes, took a deep breath, and then focused on bringing her energy back to gentle concern.

"Melissa, I wasn't joking. I meant what I said. I hope you never have to go through what I did. You don't have to believe me, but please be careful."

"Uh...that was weird," Melissa muttered as she shifted uncomfortably. "Can we go?"

"Sure babe," Richard smiled and placed a kiss on her forehead. "See you around, Ro."

"I sure hope not." Rosario responded. Richard laughed and led Melissa away.

"That...was awesome." Wade said, his voice full of awe.

"Thanks…" Ro felt herself shaking, adrenaline beginning to wear thin. Michael wrapped an arm around her shoulder and pulled her to his side. Rosario was glad for the steadying touch.

"Well. This place is ruined." Kamala said. "Let's leave."

"Seconded." Peter responded. "Michael, where are you staying?"

"Well, I was thinking about just driving back, since there's no room for me at the inn," Michael said.

"The inn?" Wade asked. "There's a Hilton Express like--"

"It's a metaphor," Kamala laughed. "But seriously, there's a hotel like right down the road. Just crash there for the night."

"I'll split it with you," Rosario blurted out. Four pairs of eyes snapped to her.

"I don't really want to go to share a bed with my little brother," she offered. "Plus all our stuff is still in the car."

"If you're sure," Michael said after a moment, giving her a funny look. Rosario nodded and did her best to ignore Wade's quiet squeal. Rosario cut him a glare, but Wade's grin was blinding and unflinching.

"Well looks like we're going to get going," Peter says as he yanks Wade off toward their car.

"Make sure to use the presents I got you!" Wade hollered.

Kamala waggled her eyebrows before she gave them each a hug and jogged off to catch up with the boys.

Together Rosario and Michael made their way to the hotel down the road. Michael made a show of allowing them to split the bill, but it turned out they only wanted to take one credit card to hold the room,

Rosario let him have it. He grinned triumphantly all the way back to their suite and unlocked the door with a flourish.

The room was big and spacious and Rosario was *exceedingly* happy to find it had two queen beds instead of a single king. A pressure she hadn't known was building dissipated from her shoulders and she held back an audible sigh.

Michael flopped onto one of the beds face first and said into the pillows. "When Wade mentioned his presents...was he talking about condoms?"

Rosario groans and toppled onto her bed with a soft smack.

"I thought so," Michael replied.

They brushed their teeth together in silence, and sleepily climbed into bed. Just after he turned off the light, Michael stooped down to kiss Rosario on the forehead, but in the darkness, the angle became his lips on hers.

In an instant, the heat between them lit into a fire. They kissed, tangled together for long enough that Michael laying down next to her was as natural as breathing. Michael held himself carefully over her, making sure not to box her in, and Rosario slid a hand through his forever messy hair.

Rosario woke to a bright day inside the room.

"We didn't close the blinds," Michael groaned. Rosario's heart thumped hard in her chest and Michael was close enough that he was sure to hear it.

"You have *terrible* morning breath," she deflected.

Michael cracked open an eye and grinned up at her sleepily.

"Oh yeah? Well, you snore."

THE END

ACKNOWLEDGEMENTS

This book would not have been possible without the creative powerhouse of positivity that is National Novel Writing Month. It is always NaNoWriMo in my heart.

Thank you Scarlett Barnhill, my tireless editor, for taking my 30 day fever dream and hacking away at it until something beautiful formed.

Thank you to my family for their support during the times I spent writing. Especially my parents, for always encouraging my love of reading (except that one time the teacher had to call and tell you not to punish me from books.)

Thank you to Luke, my loving husband, for always being supportive of my dreams, even when I broke his heart by not setting this novel in space.

And thank you, for reading. If you've made it this far you've won a special place in my heart. This book has been a labor of love and I'm so, so happy you opened it up.

Made in the USA
Coppell, TX
02 March 2021

51131158R00098